N1

Over-worked and ill-fed, Ned and his dog, Turnboy, lead a life of misery in the kitchens of Winterpicks Manor. But with the arrival of Mr Ransom, the handsome young tutor, Ned gains a loyal friend and protector.

The future looks brighter than it's ever done for Ned, until he realises that his master's niece, Felicity, is falling hopelessly and unsuitably in love with Mr Ransom . . .

BARBARA WILLARD

Ned Only

A Magnet Book

First published in Great Britain 1985
by Julia MacRae Books
This Magnet edition published 1986
by Methuen Children's Books Ltd
11 New Fetter Lane, London EC4P 4EE
Copyright © 1985 Barbara Willard
Printed in Great Britain
by Richard Clay (The Chaucer Press) Ltd
Bungay, Suffolk

ISBN 0 416 95510 X

1

NED HEARD MRS HANNAH running as fast as her size would allow, along the stone-flagged passage to the kitchen. Her shoes slapped and her housekeeper's keys danced and jingled at her waist. Ned began to tremble. He knew what must come next.

He was not the only one. Everyone in the kitchen stopped work and swung towards the door. Mrs Hannah burst in as though giants, wild animals, devils were at her heels. Mrs Hannah was not only fat but tall, and every inch of her, from her chins to her big ankles, quivered and shook. At such moments her everyday bad temper became something worse – she turned into a fury.

"Sir Joshua!" she cried – indeed she almost shrieked it out. "The master! Coming to the kitchen! Coming to inspect! Quick! Mary – Susan! Wake up, can't you? Lucy! Peg! Everything cleared! Everything out the way! Mrs Betty – hide that brandy bottle or it'll be the worse! Clear that table, one o' you and sharp about it! Ned! *Ned*! Clean up they great drops o' grease off of the hearth! Daniel – fetch a broom, do! Mary, you slut – stir y'r lazy bones – I'll box them ears, else, see if I don't. Ahhhh! You was laughing! I see plain you was laughing!"

"Got to laugh, now'n again," Mary muttered. Then she screamed as the housekeeper grabbed her arm and swung her round and shook her till Ned thought poor Mary's head must come clean off her shoulders and spin across the kitchen.

"Old devil," muttered one of the other girls.

"I heard that, Susan. Wicked, unbiddable girl! I'll see you set t'other side a locked door – aye, shut out and shivering and snivelling and none to give crust or roof!"

The girls began to scurry about, moaning and complaining and near to tears, for the worst things they could imagine were not impossible in that household. Mrs Hannah held much power in Sir Joshua Bidgood's establishment, and from needing to keep his favour showed little favour to others. Because of this, the kitchen erupted into frenzy. Pans clattered, cupboards slammed; cloths slopped and mopped at table and stools; the floor was swept into swirls of dust.

Ned had flung himself down by the hearth. He scraped and picked at the grease that had dropped in fat tears from the meat roasting on the spit. The floor stayed warm by the hearth, with its great greedy fire that had to be for ever fed and tended. The grease had no chance to turn hard and dry but soaked into the flagstones.

"I can't nohow get it clean," Ned said to Daniel, who had paused in his sweeping. He had a kind heart and would always help Ned, who was a good deal younger. "What'll master say, Dan, when he see the mess? What'll come when he see how I let them great gouts lie?"

"There's none born can cook wi'out splashing, Ned."

"He'll have me beat for sure. He'll get Jem beat me – he will. Reckon Jem's the strongest man about here . . ."

"Ssshh! Stand up, quick. He'm come."

As the master of the house appeared in the doorway, Mrs Hannah was transformed. Her eyes cast down, her hands crossed at her waist, such as it was, she dropped a careful curtsy.

From long custom, for Sir Joshua's inspection of the kitchen was a familiar ceremony that might take place at any time without warning, the rest of the servants hustled into line a pace or two behind the housekeeper. Mrs Betty, the cook, seldom at her best by this time of day, was supported nervously by two of the girls; the rest quickly found some sort of order. Rising from her curtsy, Mrs Hannah looked quickly over her shoulder at the rest and sharply nodded. Obediently, every girl bobbed. Daniel, and Stephen, who was footman and worked mostly in other parts of the establishment, bowed

6

low. Ned did his best to copy them. He was by now shaking so much that he was even more likely to fall over than the cook. Nothing in Ned's fourteen years had been very comfortable or seemed likely to become so; but above all else he dreaded his master's visits to the kitchen.

Sir Joshua stood in the doorway, surveying them all like a general accepting a salute; like a king acknowledging his subjects, his slaves, who cringed before him.

"Good day to ye all," he said at last. His voice was harsh and dominating. It was a voice to startle, to alarm. It came from a small body that seemed almost stuffed into its good clothes, and from a square-jawed, rather large face entirely without humour, sympathy or charm.

"Sir," said Mrs Hannah, almost in a whisper, "good day also to you, master."

His gaze now ranging slowly over the company before him, Sir Joshua drew from his pocket a fine cambric handkerchief which at last he raised to his high-bridged nose in a casual bundle. He lifted his chin slightly, as slightly wrinkled his nose, sneezed violently. Then the sound of his nose being ceremonially blown trumpeted throughout the kitchen. The sound, Ned thought, must surely reach as far as the parlour, even the bedchambers.

"Ahhhhh . . ." Clearly that sneeze had been a sneeze of the first order. Sir Joshua almost smiled. Then returning the handkerchief to his pocket, he nodded slightly to Mrs Hannah. "We will proceed. Tell me first of all how that boy progresses in his duties."

And as with great dignity he subsided on to the stool Daniel had hurried to place for him, he pointed slowly and solemnly at Ned.

SIR JOSHUA BIDGOOD had not always been the master of such an establishment as Winterpicks Manor, set under the downs in the county of Sussex. He had been a London merchant, grown rich in various ways he was content to forget. He had hoped to be made an Alderman but had been passed over too often for his comfort. Then, when it had seemed likely that the King would return from exile to sit on his father's throne of England, Joshua Bidgood had lent extravagantly to the Royalist cause in hope of reward. A costly business; and it had not brought him the civic eminence he had dreamt of. He was granted a knighthood and an estate in token of the royal gratitude. The estate was a shabby one, the manor house half-tumbled, the land in near ruin from years of neglect. It took another small fortune – his first wife's – to set things to rights. Now, some years later, he lived in comfortable state, though the gentry in those parts were not much inclined to notice him.

"The time shall come," he would often say complacently. For he had his plans . . .

With Sir Joshua at Winterpicks there lived his second wife, much of an invalid. There was one son of this marriage, though none of the first. Master Robert Bidgood was fifteen. There was also Sir Joshua's ward, his first wife's niece, Felicity Skelton, a few years older than her cousin, Robert. This young lady was a most valuable member of the household. She was heiress to a quite comfortable fortune. When Sir Joshua arranged a marriage for her, to some husband of wealth and title, he would, by the terms of his guardianship, reap immense benefit. In fact it was with such an event in mind that he so often said, "The time shall come." He saw his ward, no doubt, as at the least the wife of an earl and he imagined himself transported into high society. "My niece the countess . . . My nephew-in-law the earl . . ." What a triumph!

Tales of the family and the life they led day by day were brought to the kitchen by Stephen, who often rode out in attendance on Sir Joshua, by the valet, Henry, or by Lucy and Peg, who looked after the bedchambers and sometimes did small personal services for Mistress Felicity – Lady Bidgood had her own attendant.

It took a great many servants, indoors and out, men and women, working hard by day and often by night in every season of the year, to supply the needs of this household of

8

five. The house had to be cleaned, the fires lit, the food cooked, the linen laundered, the clothes mended. The horses had to be cared for, the harness and the coach well kept, the dogs kennelled and good vegetables grown. And there was the farm, too, with cowmen and ploughmen, shepherds, dairy-maids, henwife; and a man whose sole care was the team of oxen that pulled the plough and brought the harvest home. That was Jem, whose heavy hand Ned dreaded. There had to be a French maid for her ladyship; and, just lately, barely a week ago, there had arrived a tutor for Master Robert.

And of all these serving people dependent upon Winterpicks, none was humbler than Ned, the kitchen boy, who stood trembling as Sir Joshua raised his hand and pointed, saying, "Tell me first of all how that boy progresses in his duties."

'That boy' had, before all else in his life, to keep the spits, with their great roasting joints of meat and chicken and geese, turning evenly before a fire kept bright, hot and clear. There can be no better way of roasting meat than this, and Sir Joshua insisted that no other way be used. Ned did not actually turn the spit with his own hands – in a way it was worse than that. It was his place to see that another being never flagged in the task. The spit was turned by a small dog, treading round and round through a wheel that set the whole device in motion. This ancient machine had been in the Winterpicks kitchen for long years before Sir Joshua Bidgood came to the place but he would not hear of replacing it. So on and on and round and round the little dog went, thirsty from the heat of the fire, the luscious meats turning just out of his hungry reach, allowed no respite till the meat was ready to be sent to table.

In the Winterpicks kitchen the dog was called *Turnboy*. He was not the first to have carried the name, for the work had worn out several predecessors. Turnboy, this Turnboy, was fortunate in only one particular. He had a staunch and devoted friend. Ned was that friend, who would defy even

Mrs Hannah if that made Turnboy's life any easier. And at night, when Ned slept on a heap of old sacks piled under the kitchen table, Turnboy crept in beside him; and if they also shared one another's fleas – who was to say whether Ned's fleas or Turnboy's bit the harder?

"Well, boy? Come, now, boy," said Sir Joshua, in that big hard voice that seemed to come right up out of his breeches. "How are things with you, boy? Do you work as you should? Do you pay your debt to me in honest service? When you say your prayers do you remember to give thanks for a good master?"

Ned stood trying to look up at that master, which was not very far, but his eyes would travel no higher than the gentleman's stocking-tops.

Mrs Hannah gave him a shove, her hand in the small of his back.

"Answer, can't you?"

"It is ever so, my good soul," Sir Joshua said, smiling sadly at Mrs Hannah. "Those that needs most be grateful are the least likely to give thanks." He was carrying his cane, ebony with an ivory knob, and he slid it across the floor and prodded Ned's feet, so that he hopped. "Forgotten even your name, have you, boy? Well, so have I. So have I – and need you and none other to remind me." Again he prodded. "What's your name? Your name! Your name!"

One of the girls giggled nervously and Mrs Hannah swung round to glare. This scene had been played out so often that everyone knew how it was bound to go. Mrs Betty actually yawned.

"Come – come, come!"

"Ned, sir . . ." Ned had to clear his throat, for the words would never come when he needed them. "N-Ned, sir."

"Ned. Ned what?"

Now Ned was shaking with nervousness. His parents had found the courage to run away from Winterpicks and the tyranny of Sir Joshua; but they had left their only child helpless behind. Ned had been forbidden ever to speak his father's name, or to use it as his own, and it was the master's cruel delight never to let the boy forget this.

"What else?" he demanded now. "We needs must have at the least two names to take us through life. Two is considered enough for the lower kind of person. What's your second name, simpleton?"

"It's Ned only, sir."

"Ah! At last. Well, well, Master Ned Only – here's a state of affairs. What can come to a fellow so called – unless he's so happy as to find Christian lodging in a good man's household?"

"As so he has, sir!" cried Mrs Hannah as she always did at this point. "What better roof than yours, dear sir – what better master for one of life's unfortunates?"

"Then have you nothing to say to me, Ned Only? Have you no thanks? Do you not owe your very existence to my bounty? And have you no thanks?"

"I don't rightly be sure – " Ned began.

"You *don't rightly be sure?* Then let you learn your lesson now. You live by my charity, Ned Only, as do all those present here in this kitchen and many beside in stable and dairy. And see how modest these stand, all ready to give honour where honour is indeed due. I'll be bound they're ready. How say you, Mrs Hannah?"

"Why, yes – yes, sir, good sir – indeed they do daily pay that honour." She raised her hands, as if she were about to pray, and cried to all the rest, "Now thank him! Thank this good master from the bottom of your wretched hearts for all he done and give . . ." Her voice suddenly sharpened and she snapped out, "Say after me: God bless and thank our good master!"

There came a great uneasy gabbling, words tumbling over words, two of the girls actually breaking into sobs that sounded almost hysterical. It was as if every one there had been struck anew by the wretchedness of their situation. They knew too well that they were indeed dependent on Sir Joshua and could hope for no wage save chill charity. Every one had come into that household through some personal disaster, even those who had come to Winterpicks after service with Sir Joshua in London. Mrs Hannah had been deserted by her husband, Mrs Betty's man had gone off to sea; two of the girls had been cruelly orphaned, another turned from home by her stepfather . . . Stephen's whole family had died of the plague; Daniel had seen his father hanged for stealing a sheep and his mother had died of sheer bitter shame . . . And so it went on, indoors and out; even the dog, Turnboy, had been taken in after being found injured and lost.

Sir Joshua listened with apparent satisfaction to the clamour. He recognised himself as a noble benefactor, and so, in a way, he was. But the submission he demanded in return was a high price that they knew they must pay or find themselves thrown out on a world not kind to deserting servants. Who else would employ such untrustworthy creatures?

"Send one of the wenches for Mr Ransom, my good soul," Sir Joshua now ordered Mrs Hannah. "Tell him to step this way. He should learn what sort of a household he has entered."

Mr Ransom was the tutor, so recently come to have charge of young Master Robert's studies.

"Go sharp about it, Lucy," Mrs Hannah cried. "Mr Ransom, girl. The master orders his presence here."

Lucy scurried off and while they waited Sir Joshua improved the time by telling his servants yet again how beholden to him they were, how they must starve without his bounty and freeze to death should he deny them shelter.

"Ah!" he cried at last, seeing Mr Ransom at the door.

"Sir?" said Mr Ransom, glancing from side to side, surprised, no doubt, at being summoned to the kitchen. "How can I serve you, sir?"

He was tall and stood very upright. He was young and he was handsome, so that every woman there gazed on him with pleasure, even Mrs Hannah herself. His clothes, suitably plain for a man in his situation, were dark brown like his hair and eyes. He looked more of a gentleman than might be expected of a tutor in such a country establishment as this one.

Here was a good moment, Ned thought, to shuffle away and hide himself among all the rest. Daniel would stand in front of him and help his concealment.

"Wait!" bellowed Sir Joshua, attracted by the movement. He flung up his hands as if in total despair. "I ask you, Mr Ransom – what should be done with such a lad? This is he we call Ned Only, a waif deserted by his abominable parents and living ever since on my charity. And he tells me he *didn't rightly be sure* about the matter. As a man of experience in dealing with young lads – what should be done with such a ruffian?"

Ned stared wildly at the tutor and Mr Ransom very slowly looked him up and down. Ned had never any colour in his cheeks but now he felt as if all the blood in his body were slowly draining away. He could not stop his trembling. What punishment might the tutor be considering? What beatings and starvings was he going to suggest?

"Well? Well? Speak up, Mr Ransom."

Mr Ransom looked Ned over yet again. Then he spoke.

"He is very thin," he said.

There was a second's incredulous silence. Nothing was heard in the kitchen but Sir Joshua's breathing, coming fiercely through flaring nostrils and increasing in volume most alarmingly.

"Thin, sir?" he cried at last. "*Thin*? What's thin? What does that mean – *thin*? I made no query as to his *size*!"

"I beg your pardon," said Mr Ransom. "It is just that his thinness strikes me before all else." His manner was utterly courteous, the firmness of his words exactly matching his easy, pleasantly pitched voice.

"Some boys are thin and other boys are – well, not so thin," said Sir Joshua, spluttering slightly.

"That is certainly true, sir," agreed Mr Ransom, with a respectful smile. "I take Master Robert to be much of an age with this lad; but though I would not call him fat, I would not call him thin." Now his smile was for Ned. "Could this boy not be persuaded to eat rather more?"

"Eat more? He is here to work – not to eat more."

"But should he be persuaded to eat more," the tutor insisted, "might he not also work more?"

"Pish!" shouted Sir Joshua. "I brought you here to show you the orderly working of my household, not to invite your impertinence. I am not to be trifled with, sir, as you shall most certainly discover. You will stay to witness that I am firm with underlings and will suffer no defiance. There is a matter in hand here which may cause you to think carefully." He banged on the floor with his cane, then swung it in the direction of Ned. "Away with you – *thin boy*."

Ned scuttled for cover, slipping quickly in behind Daniel, who was always his friend. As he did so, he knew that there was a sudden change among all the others clustered there. A hint of anticipation, of fear, ran from one to the other. The girls caught one another by the hand, shrinking back as though to make room. And in moving they left the footman, Stephen, in some manner isolated, standing on his own and waiting for what might be to come.

Sir Joshua once more looked his servants over in silence, settling himself more comfortably on the stool, flicking imaginary particles from his coat sleeve and generally delaying whatever it was he planned to say next.

Ned whispered to Daniel, "What's Stephen done, then?" But Daniel only frowned and shook his head.

"I understand," Sir Joshua said at last, "that one among you seeks my counsel. Is that correct, Mrs Hannah?"

"Aye, sir. Stephen Tuppen, sir. Wishes to gain your kind attention."

"Then, Stephen Tuppen, you may address yourself to me at this convenient moment." He glanced up at the tutor. "You shall see," he promised. "You shall see."

Stephen stepped forward. He cleared his throat.

"Sir . . ."

"I trust you make no long petition, Tuppen. To the point.

14

And let it be a sharp one."

Now there was a deep silence in the big kitchen. Not even the fire stirred or dropped so much as a thimbleful of ash. Almost all of them there knew what Stephen was going to say, and many of them were as nervous as he was. Among the girls, Peggy stood, very white, holding on to Lucy's hand.

"Sir," said Stephen again, standing with his chin up and his feet a little apart, as if to be certain the good ground was there to keep him upright. "Sir, it is a simple matter and need not delay your honour too greatly. Peggy there, master. Her and me's took a fancy to get wed."

Even Mrs Hannah, Ned thought, was holding her breath. Every gaze was bent on Sir Joshua. Not even he could have hoped for more attention. He was hardly an easy man to ask for a blessing, but what could there be to trouble him in two of his servants wishing to become man and wife? And yet how anxiously they all awaited his reply . . .

It came in a low voice, the distant rumble of approaching storm. At the sound, despair came into the kitchen like a presence.

"Have you lost your wits, Tuppen? Am I to support a *family*? Shall I have the charge of feeding and clothing a pack of miserable, bawling brats? And for no better reason than that two of my servants have *took a fancy*?"

"Master, you know well I work hard. I can work harder."

"I'll hear nothing of it. Mrs Hannah – Peggy is to go. See to it – and by tomorrow morning. Send her off. Send her off, the strumpet!"

He was on his feet. The stool tumbled. He struck at it with his cane as if it were his enemy. Nobody spoke or so much as stirred. No one dared drag up one word of fear, of hatred, of appeal.

"See to it!" he shouted again. "See to it!"

He turned, thrusting Mr Ransom out of his path, and stumped from the kitchen.

For a second Mr Ransom stood utterly still. He was very pale. Then he moved. He crossed to Stephen and held out his hand.

It was so unexpected, so extraordinary, that everyone gasped and then the silence broke apart. Peggy began to sob and wail and the others crowded round her, Lucy and Mary weeping with her. It was the strangest thing that Ned had ever seen – a man of Mr Ransom's sort offering his hand to such as Stephen Tuppen . . .

"We are both servants of the same master," he heard Mr Ransom say, "but he too must answer for his actions. Take heart."

He looked round at them quickly, touched Ned on the shoulder and smiled slightly, then followed after Sir Joshua.

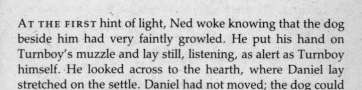

2

AT THE FIRST hint of light, Ned woke knowing that the dog beside him had very faintly growled. He put his hand on Turnboy's muzzle and lay still, listening, as alert as Turnboy himself. He looked across to the hearth, where Daniel lay stretched on the settle. Daniel had not moved; the dog could only have been disturbed by mice or rats, scuttling across the floor to forage in corners.

Then Ned realised that Daniel, quiet as he lay, was as wide awake as any man could be. Still as a log, he was listening, waiting for a following sound. Then he stiffened as a door creaked, the heavy old door that opened into the yard.

Ned sat up, still quieting the dog, who quivered with impatient longing to fill his lungs and bark.

"Ssshhh . . ." Daniel whispered, as quiet as a sigh. He swung his legs over the edge of the settle and stood up, waiting.

The door opened a foot or two, letting in a streak of early light. Stephen, who slept over the stables on the far side of the yard, slid into the kitchen. He peered towards the fire, searching out Daniel, who spoke his name very quietly. Stephen went to him and spoke in an urgent murmur that Ned was only just able to hear.

"Dan – you must tell Peg. I'm waiting in the church porch."

"The master never said you was to be sent off."

"I'm to stay – while Peggy goes? That's likely! Now listen, do. Don't fail me. Give the message I tell you. We'll needs get away sharp – no time to miss and go seeking. The church porch, Dan. Say I'm there till she come after me."

"What'll come to you? How'll you live? Where'll you get to, friend?"

"I'll get where I'm sent. There's a letter. He give me a letter."

"He? Who's that? Who's *he*?"

"Mr Ransom. Who else'd care? He come to the stables last eve and give me this paper. It's writ to his brother. I'm to take and give it to his brother. My brother'll give you work, he says – he'll take care o' you and your good girl . . . Them was his words."

"He seem quite a gentleman – and he'll do so much for a servant?"

"You heard what he said. Servants of the same master – meaning he were a servant as much as me."

"Aye, he did say so. It's a wonder to me," Daniel said. He frowned. "How far?"

"Into Kent. A long step. Go north-east, was what he said – get to the forest where there's good cover – good hiding. Ask at the *Black Ox*, he said . . . They'll set me on my way, see?"

"Let you never lose that letter."

"I'll be dead before any takes that," Stephen said and he sounded grim, "and any's dead that tries it." He touched Daniel's arm. "Best I get on before any calls for me. No use in doddling here. Farewell, Daniel."

"Farewell Stephen – good friend Stephen. Be sure I'll see Peg finds you."

Stephen paused by Ned, cuffed him lightly and ruffled his dusty hair. Then he was gone, and they could only stare after him and pray that all might go well.

The dog, Turnboy, too, stared at the closing door. He whined gently. It was as if he knew well enough that he had had three friends and now he had two. But three or two, the one he needed most was Ned Only, who stole scraps for him, who raced through the woods with him in those few moments of freedom they were allowed from the tyranny of work. Then Ned would shout and yell and Turnboy bark in mad delight. He was a sturdy short-legged brown dog – a little lame in his left hindquarter but not enough to hinder his fun. He belonged to that breed, one of the farm men had said, that the drovers used to drive their cattle. They would come out of Wales and make the long journey across England, taking their beasts to market in London and beyond. Maybe Turnboy had been such a cattle dog, alert, bright-eyed and strong. And maybe, when his leg was injured, he got left behind, and so wandered, limping and bedraggled and lost, until he came to Winterpicks . . .

Stephen was barely gone when the house stirred. The sleepy maids came into the kitchen to begin the day, with Mrs Hannah fussing behind them and Mrs Betty with her, pulling at the laces of her grubby stays that she wore like a lady but which had never seen the wash-tub. What with that and her gap-toothed gums as she yawned, poor Mrs Betty was an unlovely sight. Ned could hardly bear to look at her. He grabbed up Turnboy and rushed out of doors.

There the fine morning was spreading up the sky and the birds had already broken into scattered song. There were sounds of milking from across the yard as Ned dashed on his way with Turnboy at his heels. Turnboy had affairs of his own to attend to, and so, too, had Ned. They left the yard and ran up the neighbouring field, then into the next that was rough untended ground with a small birchwood trimming its crest. All this land rose gradually to the south, striving to become a part of the downland.

At the edge of the wood a spring ran over a stone outcrop and fell into a chalky basin of its own making. Ned tossed the bright water into his eyes and then scooped up the next handful to drink. Turnboy, too, drank at the spring, shaking the drops from his head and whiskers, scratching with enjoyment. After that there was nothing for it but to stretch and sigh and go snudging back together to the long day's toil in the manor kitchen.

But the year was turning. The hazels and the birches were tasselled and fringed with catkins; there was clarity in the morning sky that was a sure farewell to winter. And when the days indeed lengthened, there would be more time for Ned and Turnboy to scour the countryside for adventure . . .

As they reached the yard there came a great commotion, half babble, half shouting. Men and maids alike were clustered near the kitchen door, through which Mrs Hannah was leading Peggy. Leading was perhaps not quite the word. The housekeeper had the girl by the arm and was dragging her, tugging her away from the only companions she knew, who surged forward to say goodbye.

"Stand back all! Leave her go. Leave her go in silence, like she deserve – the huzzy! Making eyes at the men! I'd think shame to it, that I would."

Ned stood with Turnboy in the field and looked down on the miserable scene. As Mrs Hannah shouted, and struck out with her free hand, the girls fell back, wretched and angry, while Peggy struggled to escape Mrs Hannah's grasp. She carried a very small bundle; all she owned in the world, no doubt, and maybe half of that made up of crusts pressed upon her by the others.

"Where'll I go? Where'll I go?" Ned heard her crying. "Where's Stephen that loved me? What come to Stephen that he never got to say farewell?"

"Ah, my girl, now you see that all men are false rogues! He's snug and warm in the straw, I shouldn't wonder, and will not show his lying face."

At that Ned longed to shout out that Stephen waited in the church porch, that they'd soon be away together . . . And where was Daniel who was to have given her the tidings?

Ned watched in anguish as Mrs Hannah, with a sudden great shove, sent Peggy stumbling out of the yard and into the lane, the gate slamming behind her. Now poor Peg was out in the world indeed, and all the rest imprisoned and helpless. For a second she stood holding out her hands as if, even now, there might be some mercy . . . Then she turned, and with head bowed and tears falling, she moved on her way.

Ned turned back into the field and began running along the hedgerow, stooped double for fear he might be seen. He must get out into the lane at the next gate and tell Peggy what Daniel clearly had failed to, for she was walking in the wrong direction. From the front of the manor house, a tree-lined avenue ran towards the main gate, sloping a little downhill and coming at last to the church. Peggy had chosen to take the opposite direction, which would lead her eventually to the town some miles away. Then, as he reached the field gate, Ned saw that Daniel was ahead of him. He had stopped the girl, and giving her a quick hug had spun her round and pointed towards the church.

For a second Ned hardly dared breathe. She appeared bent on going her own way. Daniel argued and pulled at her arm but still she shook her head; perhaps Mrs Hannah's harsh words had made her doubt Stephen ... In despair, Daniel seized her and shook her – and suddenly she seemed to understand. She broke from Daniel and began to run. Fast and faster she ran, helped on by the incline, getting smaller and smaller to Ned's eagerly watching eyes.

And then he felt as if the sun had burst out in midday warmth and brilliance. He saw Stephen run from the porch and catch Peg in his arms. Then they were hurrying away together. Distance removed them utterly from Winterpicks.

"They got away," Ned said, crouching by Turnboy and speaking close by his ear. "Shall us'n go after'm one day? Shall us?"

He imagined a fine early morning, dawn scarcely broken, the two of them striding off together, never stopping until Winterpicks was no more than a speck on the horizon and all that lay ahead was unknown.

THE WHOLE MANOR, parlour to kitchen, farmyard to stable, was shaken by Sir Joshua Bidgood's rage when he learnt that he had been defied. He shouted for every available man about the place and ordered them to make a hue and cry after the pair of lovers. Sure enough, they set out with cudgels and staves and bloodthirsty cries, as if to make a settlement with robbers and murderers. They returned long after midnight, by which time the pair would have been far away.

The master was waiting up.

"Well? Well?"

"No news, your honour – never a trace. Never a soul seen 'em, nor could tell of any as might've."

Sir Joshua's colour was alarming. He controlled himself somehow and dismissed the searchers.

"Their sins shall find them out," he was heard to say to Mr Ransom.

What the tutor replied none knew, but they went to their beds shaking with triumphant laughter.

Two short in the household meant more work for the rest. Daniel was given Stephen's job, and this was promotion indeed. It made him nervous and short-tempered with the rest, but even Mrs Hannah encouraged and praised him. Ned now did most of Daniel's work as well as his own. He had still to care for the hearth, see the spit kept turning, cart the dirty dishes to the pump and keep the kitchen floor swept. But now he had also to chop wood and carry in logs, humping the great baskets that were almost as tall as he was, and a good deal thicker round. And these he had to struggle with, not only for the kitchen but for the parlour, the study where Robert Bidgood and Mr Ransom dealt in the weighty matters of education, the hall, even the bedchambers; though the actual bestowal of wood for those fires was taken over by Sir Joshua's valet, Henry. When he set about renewing the manor house, Sir Joshua had had a great many chimneys installed; they clustered together impressively above the gabled roof.

Each morning, now, when the house stirred soon after sunrise, Mrs Hannah would call Ned with the same words:

"Now then, you Ned there, take them logs to their rightful hearths before you stir another finger. Then see the ashes blown and the fires mending. Don't dare come away before there's flame enough to warm your hands. And keep out the master's sight – he's no way to be put in mind o' them villains that bolted from this place. Now you set about what you're here for."

There was no time to run across the fields with Turnboy and barely time to wash and do whatever else was necessary. Certainly there was no time to eat. It was bad enough getting the baskets indoors; getting them to the other rooms involved a mighty effort, since all but the hall were above stairs. Ten steps and then a right-hand turn; ten more and there, across a wide landing, was the parlour door. Ned's daily fear of being discovered by his master before all his tasks were done, took away his breath and made his heart hammer. Hunger added to his distress.

By the sixth morning of his new duties, Ned was no easier and no quicker. It was a fine day, the first of April, All Fools' Day. Ned could not even hear the birds singing because of the thumping in his ears. He stood for a moment leaning against the parlour doorpost. How to make the effort required to open the door and drag the logs into the room. . . ? As he stood there, panting, a terrible thought came into his mind. It was that now he was being driven as he himself was obliged to drive poor Turnboy at his task of keeping the spit turning and turning – and turning . . . The thought was so terrible that it brought a great sob into his throat. It sounded to him as loud as a shout and he was instantly aware of someone watching and listening, then breaking into a jeering laugh.

"Cry, baby, cry!" a boy's voice chanted. "Stick a finger in your eye!" Ned peered back, over his shoulder, and there was Master Robert Bidgood, leaning on the stair rail one flight above and aiming his catapult. "How if I give you something to cry about? I could put your stupid eye right out with this. I could. I've a good aim."

"Nay – " Ned began in a croaking voice.

"Nay – neigh – bray . . . Are you a donkey? What's your stupid name?"

"Ned . . ."

"There you are, what did I say? You *are* a donkey. Go on, donkey. Let's hear you neighing and braying or I'll shoot at your big ears. That'd help you make a proper donkey noise, eh Neddy?''

"I've to see the logs to the parlour – and there's the fire must be tended.''

"Aren't you the kitchen boy? *Sir*! You must call me *sir*, you lout. And what's such as you doing above stairs? Come to steal, have you? Wait till I tell my father!''

"The logs – sir. I did tell I'm to take 'em to the hearth – ''

Robert Bidgood, who was so much better fed, came sliding down the banister and stood by the basket. Ned tried to feel hopeful. Perhaps he would help carry it? Perhaps all the rest had been just silly teasing. . . ?

"Lord,'' cried Robert, kicking at the basket, "what a great heavy monster. You donkey to carry it! You're too small and skinny. Stand back and I'll show you who's stronger.''

Ned stepped aside, almost ready to smile, for in spite of his manner, Master Robert's face could not be called an evil one.

Instantly, Robert heaved at the basket, and with a shout of "April Fool! April Fool! Away with it, Neddy!'' he tipped the basket over on to its side, so that the logs burst forth and seemed to fling themselves down the stairs. Thumping and thudding, they bounded from step to step. The house echoed to the sound. Doors were opened and voices cried out, "What's amiss? Is the roof falling? What's to do?''

Robert Bidgood gave a great bellow.

"Quick! Help! Help! He'll kill me!''

He snatched up a couple of logs and hurled them at Ned, who took one in the stomach and doubled up. Robert was sliding away down the next flight, and as he reached the newel post he flung himself off and somersaulted in a great clumsy heap among the logs and lay among them, shouting as though he had broken legs, arms and every other bone in his body.

From below came Daniel, Lucy, Mary. From above came her ladyship's French maid, Minette, shrieking her alarm. From across the wide landing came Sir Joshua's man, Henry, with a lather-covered razor in one hand and a towel in the other . . .

Ned could not speak. The log that had winded him had then bounced painfully on his instep; the second had bloodied the back of his right hand. He shrank against the wall, shaking with fear of what would happen next, terrified that at any moment Sir Joshua himself might appear.

Mary and Lucy, now joined by Susan, broke out into cries of outrage, but whether against Ned or against Master Robert it was not easy to know. Daniel shoved by them, but could not get to Ned because of the boy rolling at the bottom of the stairs, and because of the logs, which continued to bounce in endless, numberless flight from step to step.

Sir Joshua's shout was heard from his own chamber:

"What's amiss? Henry! Come back here, you fool, and get the soap from my face."

Henry glanced over the banister, smirked to see young Robert laid low, and went back to his master. "It is nothing, sir," he said as he closed the door. "Children's games."

At the same instant Ned, his eyes tight closed as if he would escape everything by seeing nothing, heard the quick rush and rustle of some woman's dress. A warm but immensely firm voice called out,

"Robert! Be silent! I know your tricks. If your back's broken, no doubt it serves you right. But you sound very well and healthy to me."

Ned opened his eyes a slit. He saw Mistress Felicity, Sir Joshua's niece and ward, sweeping towards him. She appeared so full of purpose that he shut his eyes again, hard, and hunched his shoulders, waiting for a blow. Instead his wrist was caught and his hand, now dripping blood, held up as if for all to see. He opened one eye and saw her face, angry and beautiful.

"The poor child's bleeding!" she cried. "Lucy – fetch me warm water. Bring it to my room. Will you be silent, Robert, you great bully. I saw what happened."

"It was a joke, cousin. An All Fools' Day joke."

"I can tell you who's the bigger fool . . . Ah – there you are, Mr Ransom. Kindly take your pupil away from here."

25

Ned did not know what Mr Ransom answered, for he was entirely occupied in attending to the lady. She smiled at him, asked his name.

"He's Neddy the donkey," Robert shouted, in a last effort to hold her attention. "Ee-haw! Ee-haw!"

"What's your name?" she asked again, unmoved.

"Ned. Ned Only, Madam."

She half smiled, half frowned. "That's a strange name."

Ned seemed then to float on clouds. Anyone living would be bound to call Felicity Skelton a pretty creature, but to Ned at that moment she seemed an angel, bathed in some heavenly light which increased and almost blinded him as she put her hands on his shoulders and shoved him gently along the passage to her own chamber. Now they were at her door; now Lucy was there with a pitcher of steaming water. But from somewhere much too near at hand came Mrs Hannah's raised voice.

"What's he done now, the brat?"

"If you mean my cousin, Mrs Hannah, he has behaved like a villain."

"Your cousin, ma'am?" cried Mrs Hannah, flustered. "Master Robert? But I see you are teasing. Just let me at that lad you've hold of and I'll soon see him sorry!"

The door was open. Lucy was waved inside and Ned pushed after her.

"Thank you, Mrs Hannah," said Mistress Felicity; and closed the door in her face.

THE ROOM WAS not large, but the sun was in it, and anyway Ned had not yet had any occasion to consider the size of rooms.

"Pour the water, Lucy, and hold the bowl for me. Now, Ned, I think this may hurt you for it is a nasty raw place. I must see that that great log left no splinters. Try to keep your hand steady. Put the bowl down now, Lucy, and bring me some linen from the closet – there are torn strips of an old chemise in the little drawer on the right."

26

Ned would not have cried out or pulled his hand away if it had hurt ten times as much. He did not look at the bloodied place, for he was taken up with watching the lady's face, and listening carefully to what she said; for she talked to him all the time, as she might to a frightened pony.

"I have seen you about the place, Ned. But now it is different, for I know your name. Your hands are very dirty, you know, Ned – but then, no doubt, so is your work. What else do you do beside bring up the logs?"

"Chops 'em. Strips the bark a bit. Then I'm the turnspit, madam. Only it'd be Turnboy does the most work."

Lucy laughed at this, but the lady frowned.

"What does he mean?"

"Turnboy's the dog, ma'am – the dog that runs in the wheel as turns the spit mostly. You might say he'm Ned's dog, for Ned do care for'm and find bits of food and such."

Again she frowned, and glanced up from Ned's tattered hand to Ned's face.

"Poor dog," she said. "Poor boy." And then she said, half to herself. "Why do I know so little? Have you been long about this work, Ned?"

He nodded. It seemed forever since he had lived with his mother and father in the cottage at the back of the farm, since that morning when he woke alone and ran crying to the big house; since he had heard Sir Joshua saying, "And now you shall work for your keep, as is right and proper. Your gratitude and service shall be for me, your master, who refrains kindly from sending you off after those ingrates, your abominable parents. May they starve at the roadside for their treachery."

He meant, of course, their treachery to him, who had brought them into his household to assist in his grand designs, not their treachery to their only child . . .

"You tell me, Lucy. Has Ned worked here long?"

"Since he come like an orphan, mistress. How old then, Ned?"

He shook his head, unsure, vaguely ashamed.

"A little boy," Lucy explained. "Not a lad like now – which must be fourteen year, more or less. He'd be about seven or eight year old then. Is that right, Ned?"

He mumbled something. He did not want to remember.

"There," said Miss Felicity, tying the bandage firmly. "Tell Mrs Hannah I shall expect to see that hand in the morning. Make sure he comes to me, Lucy." She smiled in a reassuring manner. "You can go now, Ned."

3

LIFE CHANGED for Ned. There was still the kitchen, still the hearth and the spit and the logs; but Miss Felicity never forgot to smile when she saw him, and Mr Ransom would always call *Good day*, and sometimes stop and prod his ribs to see if he had grown a little less thin, so that there was a good laugh between them. Once or twice Ned had noticed Master Robert watching him from some distant place – beyond the yard gate, from the doorway across the hall – but he made no threatening gesture, just stared without expression and then turned away. And was it even possible that Mrs Hannah, too, had changed a little in her manner towards him? Was she less harsh, her voice a tone or two milder; and could this mean that the smiles of Mistress Felicity, the jokes of Mr Ransom had given Ned some kind of blessing – almost an importance? He hardly dared think so, and he was in fact rather startled to discover himself thinking over such matters at all, thinking at all. For instead of escaping into sleep at the day's end, he would now like long awake as he dwelt on matters so unexpected and exciting. Turnboy could have told him that when he slept at last it was with a foolish, happy grin on his face . . .

Now the days softened. The frenzy of work about the Winterpicks land, the ploughing and the planting, the lambing and the calving slipped away. Now the corn was springing and they were eyeing the grass and thinking about the coming haycrop, talking of markets and consulting about the beasts most likely to do well. Ned was roused by the cuckoo, even before cock crow. Easter was long past when Daniel came to the kitchen one evening full of news.

"Any time now, the master's to set about a visit to kinsfolk."

He looked round him with pleasure at having created quite an impression. He was always the first with tales of what was happening to the family, a fact which annoyed Mrs Hannah, who considered herself privileged above all in that household.

"He never stirred abroad afore," she said. "And why should he now? I'll believe that story when he tell it himself."

"Believe as you wish," said Daniel, in the rather lofty manner he sometimes used since his promotion to more important duties beyond the kitchen. "I'll tell you all, come you'll listen. He goes into Hampshire. And there his cousin is wife to a grand and rich husband. And the place they dwell is called Ardland Court. Her la'ship is to go along too – and that thought do pester her something terrible."

"Why, poor soul, she's not the spirit nor the strength," Mrs Hannah cried. "An invalid, all but – sitting forever with her feet up and a little dog on her lap for warmth and company – and a smelling-bottle to her nose, most often."

Some agreed with Mrs Hannah's pious disapproval, but Mrs Betty cried out that it might do the lady good to be set upon her feet and made to move about like any other Christian. All, however, clamoured to hear more.

"How long shall they be away? Shall the young master go along, too? What of Mistress Felicity? She'll never be left behind?"

"Both shall stay," said Daniel, greatly enjoying himself. "Master Robert must be set fast to his studies. As for his cousin, she is to have power over all the household – meaning even you, Mrs Hannah."

"What?"

"Aye – it shall be so, I promise. For her old aunt, that Mrs Dorothea that has her house in the town, shall be fetched to keep her company and see she get to no mischief. And tomorrow I'm to ride and bring her back pillion – and what nag there is in the stable to stand her weight and mine I find hard to think."

Mrs Hannah was trembling with indignation. "Nay, nay, Daniel – you're talking to frit me. Am I to take orders from such a young lady, however rich and well bred and kind and fair in face? Much she knows of such matters." She gave a short snort of laughter, less scornful than offended. "Well, well; we'll see – we'll see." She heard one among the maids titter, and she swung round in a fury, quite her old self. "Never think you shall rest idle while the master's away! I'll see this house scoured through, roof to cellar, and them rooms that's been closed up shall be washed and dried and sweetened till the King himself might come and find no shame! And that I promise."

Just then Lady Bidgood's maid, Minette, came to the kitchen where, as her custom was, she moved with distaste, picking up her skirts lest they touch the floor and shielding her face with one delicate hand as she passed the fire.

"My lady will have hot chocolate this very minute, if you please," she said, the words heavily accented. "See to it and no delaying. Is it understood?"

"We learn that the master and mistress are to travel from home," Mrs Hannah said, at her most genteel. "Is it indeed so?"

"They go visiting in Hampshire," Minette replied. "A great house there, it is his cousin's house. And for what purpose they go," she added, her voice full of insinuations, "you shall learn one day, no doubt."

With that she left them, for she was not one to fetch or carry.

The instant the door was closed, the girls were mimicking Minette with shrieks of laughter.

"Zees minoot!" cried Lucy. "Ees eet onderstood?"

"Zey goo veesiting in 'Ampshire . . . 'is coosang's house . . ." Mary was almost hysterical, she fell into Lucy's arms and Susan rushed to join the wildly giggling pair.

"Be silent, you silly sluts!" shouted Mrs Hannah, her gentility forgotten. "Get to your work and hold your stupid tongues! Mary! You'll choke to death if you carry on so. Mam'selle Minette is quite the lady, that I am well able to recognise. You are all too ignorant to know a fine manner from a foolish!"

It took another two weeks for Sir Joshua and Lady Bidgood to prepare for their travels. They would be a month at Ardland Court, which they knew to be an elegant and sociable establishment. The necessary clothes had therefore to be assembled. Sir Joshua had wished to have new boots made in London, but Mr Ransom had advised him against it, because of the plague that had raged through the capital. So the bootmaker from the town was called in.

At last all was ready for the venture. Soon after daylight on the appointed day the entire household was clustering around the great door of Winterpicks Manor, all ready to wave Sir Joshua and his lady on their way. The great heavy coach stood waiting.

Daniel, and a couple of the farm men, ran in and out with bags and bundles packed with the paraphernalia necessary to such a visit as this was to be. The morning was quiet and overcast. Beyond and above the trees in the park, the church tower, the farm with its many outbuildings, the downs loomed like heavier, more threatening clouds. The horses stamped and chucked up impatient heads so that the harness jingled. The ostler at the leaders' heads spoke in a soft and soothing tone. The coachman mounted to the box and settled himself to wait.

Then at last there was a stir among the attendants as Sir Joshua, spruce in a new black wig, a suit almost new, and the new boots, came from the house. He was accompanied by Mrs Dorothea, his ward's old aunt, and as he went towards the coach he talked to her constantly, giving her more and more orders as to the conduct of the place while he was away.

"Your niece and mine shall advise you on all points I have not made clear. Pray have it in mind, madam, that I rely on you to guard and protect all I have left in your care."

"For sure, Sir Joshua," she kept crying. "For sure. For sure. I shall be vigilant in all things. You may indeed rely on my own good sense."

He said "H'm," adding rather insultingly, "Well, there is none other I can think of to bring here, so it must perforce be you."

She was a little less than his height but twice his girth, and she had not at all the appearance of a reliable caretaker. Ned, watching with the rest, saw Lucy nudge Susan and cover her mouth with her hand to hide her grins.

"Come now, madam, come, Lady Bidgood," Sir Joshua was crying impatiently. "If we hope to arrive we must first make a start."

Lady Bidgood had emerged, leaning on Minette's arm, holding a handkerchief to her mouth as if the very prospect of the journey induced nausea. Mrs Dorothea went to her side as speedily as she could, and with fuss and encouragement, her ladyship was stowed inside the coach, Minette with her.

Then Sir Joshua himself entered, the door was firmly shut by Daniel, who removed the block and stood back, bowing in the subservient manner expected. Henry, the valet, then climbed up on to the box beside the coachman, who twirled his whip, while the ostler looked up expectantly for the call to *Stand away*!

Whatever his feelings towards Sir Joshua, Ned could only find this grand departure very exciting. Part of the excitement, no doubt, was in the prospect of a Winterpicks free of its master ... Something brushed by his ankle and he heard a dog's whine. Had Turnboy, too, come to join the rejoicing? But it was not Turnboy at all. It was Dainty, the mistress's own small spaniel ...

The coachman had shouted to the ostler, the crack of the whip had sounded; the horses now tossed their heads to some purpose and the wheels began to turn on the driveway.

And then a fearful shriek sounded from within the coach.

Ned had no doubt at all what occasioned the shriek, whose voice it was that so wildly cried out,

"Stop! St—op!"

Ned snatched up Dainty and ran.

Now Sir Joshua's head appeared through the window, his feathered hat knocked sideways. His big voice was shouting –
"Stay! Wait! Halt, damn you!" He was still at the window, still bellowing as the coach stopped and Ned ran up with the dog in his arms.

Within the coach, out of sight, her ladyship was crying and moaning, and Minette, no doubt, had produced the smelling-salts. Sir Joshua gaped at Ned as though he could not believe the promptness of his service.

"Madam, be silent!" he called to his wife. "The dog is here. A boy has her safe." Then he peered at that boy. "Ah. Ned Only. Good. Good." He took Dainty and handed her, struggling, to his wife, then turned back to Ned. "You have obliged me," he announced. "If no other event should occur to lighten your humble life, you may assure yourself of one thing; yours has been the privilege of drying the tears of Sir Joshua Bidgood's lady."

WITH THE ABSENCE of the master from Winterpicks, the household ran quieter; just as, outside, the frenzy of spring had mellowed with the increasing summer. Old Mrs Dorothea wanted nothing better than to snooze over her embroidery by the parlour fire or by the window in the sun, and as she ate everything set before her with gusto and never went near the kitchen, she pleased Mrs Hannah. And as for Miss Felicity, whose interfering ignorance the housekeeper had dreaded, she proved a great deal more sensible than any would have expected from her lack of experience. She did come to the kitchen – but to a welcome that grew warmer as the days went by.

Now there was less work for Ned and Turnboy, for no sense could be discovered in cooking great joints for a mere couple of ladies, plus a young lad and his tutor. The evenings were long. There was freedom.

Behind the manor house, with its avenue of lime trees, its great stable block and kennels, its farm and barns and cottages, its church at the gates, was that Winterpicks land Ned found so enticing as it reached ever upward towards the distant downs. The land seemed to heave itself skyward. After a mile or so the incline dramatically increased and the goal was achieved; Winterpicks pasture became absorbed into the high bounding countryside. From the top of those galloping downs, where Ned so far had never been but knew he must one day go, there would be a new horizon. Daniel had told him of it. It was the pale line of the ocean, washing round the edge of England. When the time came for Ned to stand there, with Turnboy at his side, they would gaze westward to a high spire set where the sea ran in, and eastward to castles and cliffs. There would be time for all this one day, Ned was sure.

"At midsummer, could be," he told Turnboy. "Last summer it hardly were dark at all. There'll be time enough."

He had thought the same last year but the moment had never come.

The little wood where Ned each morning washed his face, curled round a hump of risen ground and stretched neatly and nicely out of sight of the house. The manor chimneys could just be seen from the wood's fringe and, within a nearer fold of land, the roofs of some cottages. Under one of them Ned had been born and lived with his parents, in the struggling poverty of the deserted estate, until Sir Joshua came to Winterpicks and took all into his service.

"You did bawl sore when they left you," Daniel had told Ned once.

"I misremember," Ned mumbled; for he was afraid to think of that matter . . .

Alongside the wood, in these easier days of summer, Ned had taken to building himself a fire, and there he would do a little cooking on his own account. Master Robert's catapult had filled Ned with a great desire for one of his own. Daniel had helped him make one, and Ned was fast becoming very skilled. Rabbits and pigeons, sparrows and starlings were his victims. When the birds were plucked and cleaned, the rabbits gutted and skinned, the meat was roasted at the little fire. Close by sat Turnboy, his nose twitching, his gaze flicking from the cooking meat to Ned's face.

The sun shone, the sky was fair, the trees now full and fresh. These seemed to Ned the best hours he had ever known. That was not only because of roasted rabbit and small bony birds that most wonderfully reduced his usual hunger. It was because of Miss Felicity, because of Mr Ransom. Good enough that there should be alive one gentleman like Mr Ransom, willing to offer help to such as Peg and Stephen, but that there should also be a lady, so kind and so beautiful, and the two sharing a roof with Ned himself, seemed past all understanding . . .

The master and mistress had now been from home well over a week. Ned sat whistling softly beside his fire, his thoughts much occupied with pleasant matters, and Turnboy lay stretched beside him.

"She stroke you, Turnboy, and never cried out you'd give her fleas."

She had said, when she came to the kitchen to inspect Ned's injured hand, "The dog needs care. Will you not see him washed and clean?" And as he hesitated, astonished by the request, she had added coaxingly, "Do it to please me."

Very strange, Ned had considered, to care about washing a dog – but he had shoved Turnboy under the pump the next day, and rubbed him dry with straw, as he had seen the stableboys rubbing down the horses. When it was done, Turnboy looked quite handsome. What with less work in the kitchen and bits of roasted meat, he had put on some weight. His coat already looked thicker and healthier, his eyes bright and his whole manner eager. In fact Daniel had looked at the dog and shaken his head.

"You made him too good a dog for spit-turning. He sh'd be off and about his own true work, poor fellow."

"Here's his home!" Ned cried, hating to think that Turnboy should ever be *off and about his own true work.* What if he should remember that early life – his life, as it was thought, with the drovers? What if, now he was well and eager, he ran off to seek his own old master? Or what if one day the drovers came near Winterpicks, as once before they had come to take cattle to his lordship, the High Sheriff? And suppose they were near enough for Turnboy to hear the noise the great train of animals made – the little hardy black cattle from Wales, the hundreds of geese? Then, too, he would hear and maybe answer the strange and ancient cry of the drovers themselves? 'Heiptro ho! Ho – heiptro ho!' A dog's ears are magically sharp and full of memory . . .

That day's rabbit was cooked. Turnboy's patient expectation was melting into long strips of saliva. Ned had to swallow his own spittle or he would have dribbled, too, the meat smelt so good. He tried to tear the joint into useful pieces. It was sizzling-hot and he yelped when it burnt him. He was so busy about the job, and then so anxious to blow a bit cool before handing it to Turnboy, that he had no time to realise that he was being watched.

"Ah," said a man's voice behind him, "the thin boy is taking my advice."

Ned just managed not to drop the meat as he sprang up and faced about. The grease from the roast ran over his hands and even between his dirty bare toes.

Mr Ransom stood leaning on his stick. He lifted his nose and sniffed. "How good it smells, Ned Only! Spare a sliver for a hungry brother."

Ned grinned. What things he said! He detached a hind quarter, plump and tender, and held it out on the palm of his hand. There seemed no need at all to expect everyday behaviour of Mr Ransom, so Ned did not even feel shy any more as he stood there watching the tutor chew and swallow and then lick the last flavour from his fingers one by one.

"My thanks," he said. "I'd best leave you to the rest before I seize more. You are looking a good deal heartier than when first we met, let me tell you. I am very glad to know that you listened to my advice; very glad indeed. Continue so. I anticipate even better progress."

Ned stood watching in wonder and admiration as Mr Ransom went on his way. He walked, not fast, but steadily, looking about him as he went, pausing at times to gaze up into the trees that thinned as the ground rose and then vanished over the brow of the hill. And over the brow, too, went Mr Ransom, easily pacing, his hat on the back of his head and a book sticking out of his pocket.

When the last of the rabbit had vanished inside Turnboy, Ned banged out the fire with two flat stones and set them over the ashes. He ran down the hill by the edge of the wood, with Turnboy racing alongside. He was still laughing to himself with pleasure as he recalled Mr Ransom's easy manner. Then he saw that the delights of this day were not yet done. Mistress Felicity herself was approaching the stile in the hedge that divided Winterpicks orchards from Winterpicks grazing. By the time Ned reached the stile she was halfway over, but she paused when she saw him and called out.

"Come here and lend me your hand."

He thought at first she meant the hand she had cared for after the encounter with Master Robert. It was sometimes difficult to work out precisely what ladies and gentlemen were saying, for they used strange words in curious ways.

"Come now," she insisted. "Help me or I must stay perched here until this time next week."

He dashed forward, then, and held out his hand. He wished it had been cleaner, but it seemed to serve her purpose, for she clasped it and sprang to the ground.

"Thank you, Ned. I trust all goes well with you these days?"

He nodded, rather foolishly grinning. To complete his heady pleasure, she stooped and patted Turnboy.

"He looks twice himself, the poor fellow. Have you given him a good walk? Or is it that he has given you one?"

Ned nodded at the first question and left the other to care for itself. Her attention to Turnboy was so pleasing that Ned almost blushed. Of course he knew about Lady Bidgood and Dainty, but the spaniel seemed as different from hard-working Turnboy as a fox from a hound. Perhaps all ladies felt kindly towards all dogs?

Now she was moving on her way. At last Ned found something to say. "The gentleman go that way, lady. You shall meet'un for sure."

She paused, looking back at him over her shoulder. She appeared to him more beautiful than ever. Perhaps it was because her cheeks were suddenly very pink.

THE WEATHER stayed so good that Ned was out every late afternoon with Turnboy. Once they stayed till long after the moon was up and returned to find the door barred. But there was plenty of straw in the stable and it made a better bed than Ned and Turnboy were accustomed to. When Ned's parents left him and he was taken into the kitchen, he had been forbidden, along with all the rest, ever to speak to the other children, the farm workers' families he had played with before. He had obeyed out of fear and desolation. They had soon forgotten him and he had lost the habit or the need for companions, so now he went cheerfully alone, hunting and cooking and eating and feeling no loss . . .

Two days after Mr Ransom had approved the rabbit, he passed the same way again and again paused.

"You are plumper still, since only two days. You will surely be twice yourself pretty soon. Take care though," he said, in a nicely mocking way. "Should you grow too sleek it might be thought you have been raiding the larder."

"I never would!" Ned cried. Then blushed, for he had certainly stolen food for Turnboy, and for himself. In his confusion he saw that Mr Ransom would move on his way, and he longed to keep him. But how? One way leapt happily to mind.

"Did you meet wi' the lady, master – when you come hereabouts two days gone?"

Mr Ransom indeed paused. He stood surprisingly still and looked carefully at Ned, perhaps even suspiciously. But then he seemed to change whatever had been in his mind, for he answered easily,

"We were a little time on the same path."

"I did hand her from the stile!"

"Aye – so she told me. See you stay mannerly, Ned. The world will reward you."

Now, instead of moving off, he looked towards the fire and today's meat.

"What have you to offer your guest today?"

Ned hesitated. He glanced at the triangular spit he had made. There was a chicken browning there, as Mr Ransom must be well able to recognise. Ned's easy contentment was threatened.

"It were far from the yard, master! I found 'un caught fast in brambles. It'd never get back home. One eye gone from fighting the thorns. Best dead, then . . ."

Now it would be over. Wherever he had found the bird it was manor property. Mr Ransom would be bound to tell of what was, after all, plain theft.

"It looks done to a turn, Ned. The dog's impatient. Shall we taste it?"

Relief brought actual tears into Ned's eyes.

"Shalln't you tell – ?"

"When I've enjoyed the meat myself? What are you thinking of? Come along, now. I'll have that plump left leg, if you please."

He sat down easily on the nearby bank, tilting his hat against the sunshine, snapping his fingers to Turnboy. The dog ran and pounced, then stood with ears up, taut and eager, head very slightly on one side, eyes bright with expectation.

His fingers almost trembling with happiness, Ned tore the leg from the carcase and offered it to Mr Ransom. Only one thing more could have added to the sheer wonder of the moment – if Mistress Felicity should come strolling the grassy track to join them.

He saw that Mr Ransom, his mouth full of succulent bird, had paused in his munching and was gazing down the hillside. Then he rose. In one hand he held the remains of the chicken leg; with the other he removed his hat. There was an expression on his face that Ned had seen once before, and which he recognised easily now. Just so Stephen Tuppen had looked at his love Peggy . . .

He knew without turning his head that the best had happened. She was approaching up the hill, bent towards them, bound to pause at their side. Turnboy had seen her and gone racing off.

Mr Ransom tossed away the remnant of chicken and, like a schoolboy, wiped his greasy fingers down the side of his breeches. Then he put his hand on Ned's shoulder and stood waiting, the pressure increasing as the lady came nearer and then called to them . . .

Ned had moved into another world. It was one in which these two newcomers to his life might somehow need him to give them help.

4

STILL there came no word of Sir Joshua's return, though the month was well over. Still the weather stayed soft. Each day as the end of his brief freedom grew near, Ned became fidgety and anxious. What if something happened to spoil the new order which had taken over his life with no planning at all on his part? Each late afternoon he called for Turnboy to follow and dashed for happiness. This meant lighting his fire, spitting whatever meat had come his way – and waiting. Sometimes the gentleman arrived first and sometimes it was the lady. Whichever it might be would sit down on the bank by Ned and wait for the other. And for those few minutes he had their whole attention.

Ned's wits, which had sharpened so greatly, told him that neither of them came for the joy of seeing the kitchen boy, but this did nothing to spoil things for him. His fire and his feast brought them easily together. Without him their meetings would be far harder to contrive. He was their aid and their supporter. Though they might talk all the time to one another and pay no more heed to him than to any other silly lad, he would have stayed content. But they did talk to him, they did notice him. As he grew easier with them, becoming more accustomed to their voices and better able to understand words they used which he did not, there came to be moments of laughter which all three shared.

Did anyone know of all this? The kitchen, so full of the slightest gossip, stayed silent. Once, Mrs Dorothea had been heard rather feebly scolding her niece – but none had commented on the fact. Only occasionally some remark might be made that caused a quick glance to flick from one to another. It was as if an agreement had been reached, a pact of silence been sealed, and nothing was to be said or done that might endanger the frail happiness of the pair so obviously and so unsuitably falling in love. And in a muddled way Ned knew this to be a tribute to Mr Ransom. He had helped one pair of lovers and now he should be helped in return. Even Mrs Hannah, at least in her master's absence, wished him well, though she knew, as they all knew, that nothing could come of the affair. Sir Joshua Bidgood's niece would never be allowed to wed a penniless employee of her own guardian.

So now, on yet another gentle day, Ned watched the sizzling meat, while Mr Ransom spread his coat on the bank for Miss Felicity, and then sat down beside her. Ned did not always listen to what they said to one another. He continued to tend the fire, to turn the day's prize, a plump duck wickedly lured from the safety of the pond. But when the conversation ran in general tones, then he paid attention. Already in these few weeks it was amazing to him how much he had heard and remembered. That London was fifty miles away, that the plague continued there, that there was a great church called St Paul's, while the King dwelt at Whitehall in the Palace of Westminster. Why had no one told him such things before? Now they were speaking of Winterpicks.

"The place had long been in the possession of the Shapley family," Mr Ransom was saying. "No doubt you have seen they have a tomb in the church here. It was defaced when the estate was sequestered by Cromwell; that was in Sir Anthony Shapley's time. The Shapleys were not only staunch Royalists – they were also a Catholic family."

"Alas for them, poor souls," Miss Felicity said with a sigh; but whether because they were Royalist, Catholic, or turned from their home was hard to decide. "Who came to it next?" she asked. "My uncle has never spoken of the place except as his own." She laughed and said slyly, "I think he feels it could not have existed before!"

"It fell almost to ruin after the Shapleys left – though the farm was kept up in some measure .. I had all this from Mr Langridge," he added rather quickly. Mr Langridge was the parson. "I understand Sir Joshua has been lord of this manor some few years only."

"Since the King came back to his own. You will know from Mr Langridge that my uncle's house was in London until the King honoured him. And my father's house not far. When my father died there was none to care for me. I came into my uncle's household."

"He offered you his home . . ."

"No," she said coldly. "He bought a rich ward to dispose of to his own advantage."

Mr Ransom looked quickly at Ned, perhaps wondering if he might have heard what he would repeat.

"And you, Ned Only," he said then, rather too cheerfully, as if Ned had not the sense to know the conversation was being changed, "did you, too, come from London?"

"He came here an orphan. Isn't that so, Ned? Lucy told me."

Mr Ransom shook his head at her. "Let him tell."

"Poor child – he must have been very young. You will make him sad. . . . You need not speak of it, Ned, if it distress you."

How was he to please them both?

"I am not let speak of it," he said. "So I am Ned Only." Mr Ransom was looking at him angrily, so he began to falter. "My father were ostler – and he run off. And my mother in the dairy – she run." He cried out, very much afraid of what he had said, "I am not to tell of it. Not to speak of'm. I never should've."

"Aye, indeed you should," Mr Ransom answered. "Such things are not to be forgotten. Wrongs are wrongs only that they may be righted."

This could only sound gibberish to Ned. His troubles seemed to increase because he could not understand. He must have looked very sorry for himself, for Miss Felicity cried out, "Ned! Do not look so! Here and now I will make you a promise. When I am a grand lady and have a great house, you shall come and work there. You shall not ever be in the kitchen, but in the garden and in the fields. Turnboy shall be

44

with you and have a leather collar with brass studs. He must be king of all the other dogs in the place! What do you say?"

"When?" Ned asked, his wretchedness quickly translated into joy. A whole picture of that house and garden, spreading fields, obedient dogs, rose magnificently in his imagination. "Soon, lady?" he asked.

"Nay – I cannot tell that." Her voice changed, it sharpened. "First I must be wed. No lady ever got herself a household, that I heard of – save she got herself a husband first."

Now she was laughing rather wildly, and Mr Ransom stared in a moody way at his boots. She glanced at him and then very slightly shivered, drawing nearer to the fire, spreading her hands to the warmth as if it were winter.

"You're neglecting the feast, Ned Only! That duck still looks very pale! Stir, the fire, do – or throw on more wood. At this rate we must wait till tomorrow noon. Mrs Hannah served us a meagre dinner and I am still hungry!"

The fire leapt and then settled. Ned got on with his cooking. He was disturbed by all these quick changes of voice, of mood. He could not quite turn his back on the others, knowing that they had fallen silent, that she was picking impatiently at bits of grass and daisies and then tossing them away. It was a relief when Ned could cry out, "It's ready!" and pull the duck, sizzling and spitting, from the fire, and set it down on cleaned stones, ready to be disjointed and handed round.

At once everything was easy again. The meat was not only delicious, it was scaldingly hot and this alone brought back merriment. Ned was so pleased to find that strange mood banished, to see the lady and the gentleman enjoying the results of his careful roasting, that he forgot to eat himself and left Turnboy with his tongue lolling out.

"What would your pupil say if he could see you now?" Miss Felicity cried. "You set a bad example, Master Tutor, gobbling the meat and spitting the bones and letting the grease run over your cuffs! Is this how you have taught all your earlier pupils?"

There was a slight pause. Then Mr Ransom said, "I think I have told you that your cousin is my first pupil."

45

She laughed. "And maybe your last! He is a monster."

"He is lonely, madam."

"Lonely?"

"There is none of his age for company."

"I will not be sorry for him . . . Have you indeed never been a tutor before? A scholar, then? A traveller?"

He smiled, saying that he had been his father's second son, and any second son must make his own way.

"Now my father, like yours, has died. He was a man who loved his fellows. Not many men learn that lesson. I am here to learn what he learnt – and so become as wise and kind as he. He cared for those most needing care."

"For pity's sake," she cried, "what can you learn of my cousin?"

This time he laughed. "That he is no monster but a lad alone."

"It is true," she agreed. "He is alone. But that cannot teach you – if indeed you have anything to learn."

"It was my father's word that every man, be he born as mean as the world may offer, yet has his own value that must be understood. He travelled widely when he was young, even to the New World. The Indian, he said, was his brother."

For a moment his solemnity seemed almost to frighten her, and she cried out, "Would you go so far?"

"So far as the New World – or so far as to claim an Indian brother?"

"It is a terrible journey, sir!"

Mr Ransom smiled. "Perhaps both are terrible journeys for all men. But it is the end of the journey, surely, that we strive for?"

She flushed, for he seemed to have rebuffed her – as even Ned could tell from his tone, that was gently reproving.

She said, almost sharply, "Well, sir, I am not certain that I am your pupil."

"No, no; I am the pupil. I learn from Sir Joshua, indeed, and more from Ned, here. We are all of one making. My father told me that and that is what I strive to know certainly. Winterpicks is a beginning, the start of this particular journey. It may end soon or it may end late." He looked at her earnestly. "Can you understand?"

The light was now rich with the promise of the long summer sunset. Miss Felicity suddenly sprang to her feet.

"I have stayed too long," she cried, in an agitated voice. "I was to see Mrs Langridge at the parsonage – to ask her to call on my aunt."

"Then I shall escort you," Mr Ransom said. "I wish to see the Rector who has a book he will lend me."

Ned watched them walking away down the hill. He thought the lady had come very far out of her way if she had planned to call at the Rectory. She was hurrying now and in no time had reached the stile. Mr Ransom handed her over but she seemed in too much haste even to look at him. A second more and they were out of sight, moving back into their world and leaving Ned with his own far smaller one.

All the same, he smiled to himself as he crouched by the fire, stripping the last bits of meat from the duck's carcase and feeding them to Turnboy. Turnboy would have liked the bones as well, but Ned would not give them to him – he had watched one of the farm dogs choke and die on cooked chicken bones. He scraped a hole and buried the remains, though a fox, no doubt, would dig them up again.

On the point of putting out the fire, Ned paused – then froze into stillness. There had been some movement, heavier than any bird might make, sharper than rabbit or squirrel. Ned stayed rigid, his hand on Turnboy's muzzle, straining for another sound, waiting. A second unseen movement, a snap and a tiny, whining rush of air. Something struck him on the shoulder, so that he yelped and clapped his hand to the place.

Now for the first time Ned looked upwards. There was more than one well-grown oak among the birch and hazel that made up most of the wood, and as Ned's glance went to the nearest of these, he saw who was perched in its lower branches. At the same instant, there came again that ping and

47

swish and this time a stone caught him on the ankle. The sharp pain brought tears to his eyes.

As little time ago as this morning, Ned might have run. But the company and the feasting had made him bold, the one feeding his body and the other his spirit. Now he sprang up shouting,

"Come on down, you! Turnboy! Get at'm! Get at'm, boy!"

"Send him on and I'll knock his brains out!" shouted Master Robert Bidgood.

Ned's own catapult was dangling from his belt and he seized it and fitted a stone from the handful heavy in his pocket.

"I'll knock yourn out, if you harm 'un – see if I just don't!"

"Then you'll find yourself hanged, stupid Neddy! Let be!"

Ned held his fire, not because he had any way of imagining himself being hanged for murdering Robert, but because he was surprised to see his enemy swinging down out of the oak branches. But the stone was so neatly waiting to be despatched that he could not resist letting it go. He aimed for the ground a little ahead of Robert and when it struck, it sent last year's dead leaves in a whirl about his feet. Ned let the second stone go and the third, and each time the victim leapt in the air.

"Pax!" called Robert Bidgood. He came nearer, kicking out at Turnboy, but mostly in self-defence. "Don't you know what that means, you ignoramus? Latin, stupid. Pax means stop it, and ignoramus means ignorant lout. And if you don't believe me, then you can ask your friend Mr Ransom."

Ned stood still. How long had Master Robert been in the oak tree? How much had he watched? What tale would he tell? It could only be a tale of his beautiful cousin and the tutor walking together, talking together and laughing – and only the kitchen boy for company and decent manners. Mrs Hannah, when Mr Ransom first came to Winterpicks, had called a tutor 'no more than an upper servant', and the unwed wards of gentlemen, even Ned was aware, were not intended to spend their time with such people. Master Robert would most surely report it all, not merely at once to Mrs

Dorothea, but to his father when he returned home. What fury would be unleashed? Bad enough for Ned, no doubt of that, but what of the lady herself? What of Mr Ransom? Might he be dismissed? The thought of Winterpicks without Mr Ransom filled Ned with dismay.

"Well, get on!" Robert cried. "I called Pax, you call Pax – else I'll set about you!"

"Pax," said Ned. Solitariness had taught him a certain amount of cunning. "That makes us friends, then?"

Robert hesitated. He was not without some cunning of his own. Being Sir Joshua Bidgood's only son had its disadvantages, even if it was better than working as his kitchen boy.

"I'd say – out o' doors friends," he said cautiously. "As enemies might come to be, when each is as good as t'other."

Ned frowned. The admission was acceptable but it still seemed to him to need consideration.

"Out o' doors? What's that mean?"

"What it says. Away from home, that's what it says. I'll shake your hand out of doors – but just try it under my father's roof and see what you get."

Ned's mind turned slower than the slowest turning of the spit in the manor kitchen as he tried to see the best and the worst in this arrangement. Because of what Master Robert had witnessed, he should not be angered; because of the indignity of such a mean friendship Ned's impulse was to spit on the offered hand and then to fight. Robert was bigger, but Ned was quicker . . . He remembered the talk behind him as he tended the fire: '*My cousin's a monster.*' '*He is lonely, madam.*'

Half traitor, half saviour, Ned very slowly put his hand into Robert's.

THEY RACED HOME, Turnboy far ahead, Ned leading Robert, who came panting on his heels. At that turn of the ground from which the house was first seen, both boys pulled up short. The last light shone in the windows, in the glass of the vinery, which Sir Joshua had recently added. One of the stable boys was leading away a very tired-looking grey horse.

"Who's come?" Robert cried. "I'll swear I never saw that beast before. News of my father, maybe. A courier to tell of his homecoming." There was no great joy in his voice. "Come on, Ned, don't stand gawping there like the ninny you are. Let's get on and see what's happening."

The house as they entered by the side door – Ned, unaccustomed to this, following rather nervously – was full of sound that swelled up from the kitchen, leaving all else silent and still. Mrs Dorothea must be snoozing as usual; Mistress Felicity, Mr Ransom had clearly not yet returned. It was Mrs Hannah's voice that dominated all.

"Go and see what's afoot, Ned" said Robert. "I'll not go to the kitchen – there's none there I care to talk to. Go on! And get back fast and tell me what the fuss is about."

He gave Ned a shove that sent him staggering on his way.

"Four days! Four days?" Mrs Hannah was shrieking. "And no more warning than that? And bringing guests? And who are they to be, pray, and what's their quality? Shall they come wi' their own servants to be fed and housed? Or bring none and claim service from them as is worked to death a'ready?"

All this, Ned saw, was addressed to a stranger, the owner, clearly, of the grey. He stood with his arms folded and his bottom resting on the table edge, his riding cloak tossed back, his boots dusty. His hair looked dusty, too, but in fact it was the same colour as his horse. His face, however, was not old, only arrogant.

"And who, pray, are you?" Mrs Hannah concluded. "What's your name and your quality, that you're sent to tease us?"

"I'm Samuel Kite, you silly dame – but you shall call me Mr Kite, for I'm major domo to Sir Athelstan Fitzdowne, baronet, who, dear heaven knoweth why, comes a-visiting at this meagre household. And his lady with him. And also their son, Mr Fitzdowne. And there shall be in his train also, his valet, my lady's maid and two grooms. And there's the end of my

50

message, save to see that the beds is proper, the hangings fitting, the food well planned and the entertainment sufficient."

"Entertainment!" cried Mrs Hannah, as alarmed as if the most ungodly of play-acting and dancing had been suggested. "There's no entertainment here!"

"And that, my poor soul," he answered, yawning, "is what I should expect from all I've seen. This is a low and poorish mansion, by my reckoning, and its name suits it well. For the pickings of winter is what I am most nearly reminded of as I look around me."

"Hear him!" cried Mrs Hannah, to the rest who listened, Mrs Betty, the girls, Daniel, Ned – and Turnboy, who had just slunk in. "Only listen to him! Oh that such talk should be talked under this roof! Better I died than hear it . . ."

"Peace, woman," said Mr Kite, a snap in his voice, "or there shall be a way found to stop your noise. Show me the house and where I'm to lodge. Then I'll take a bite of supper, for I've rid far enough to make up an appetite for good meat."

He bundled her from the kitchen, and two of the girls ran after, carrying candles, for the house was by now almost dusky. A twittering excitement moved all but the housekeeper, who was far too busy being outraged to have any other thought.

Ned shoved his way through the gabbling girls and went to find Robert. He was not where Ned had left him. He was by now in the hall, where his cousin had arrived with Mr Ransom still in attendance. Mrs Hannah was pouring out her tale, while Samuel Kite, now very well-mannered and respectful, nodded or shrugged or raised his eyebrows as the case demanded.

"If the master had but come home first hisself, madam! We might a' been better instructed! I take it very ill that he so mistreats us. And bold that may be, but I'm vlothered to death nearly."

"We must do our best, Mrs Hannah," she replied. "Truly,

my uncle springs a surprise – but there will surely be some good reason."

"Indeed, madam," the major domo broke in, "Sir Athelstan is a gentleman of many interests. Much occupied. Much sought after. When he finds time to spare, then for sure those who seek his company may feel much obliged."

"No doubt." Mistress Felicity's voice sounded strange to Ned, no longer warm, no longer merry; cold, rather, and strained. "See the work started then," she said to Mrs Hannah. "Show the rooms and make a choice for the guests. I must go to my aunt and tell her what's afoot. Come to me in the parlour and we will make some plan."

She moved to the stairs as Mrs Hannah led Mr Kite away. Before she had a foot on the stair, Robert was at her side and pouring out questions.

"What guests are they, cousin?"

"Did you not hear what was said? Sir Athelstan Fitzdowne. Lady Fitzdowne. Their son, Mr Vereker Fitzdowne."

"I never heard of any such – did you?"

"Oh yes. I have heard of them, Robert."

"What sort are they? Will they make good sport? Shall there be shooting? And dancing? And pray, cousin, when did you know them?"

"I knew of them before my parents died. Before I came – before I was brought to Winterpicks."

"And are they rich?" Robert persisted, more lively than Ned had seen or heard him.

"Oh yes, indeed. Very rich. Sir Athelstan has a baronetcy, though it is not a very old title. One day his son shall have it. And great estates. Wide lands."

She glanced over her shoulder as she spoke. One of the maids brought more candles just then, and Ned saw that the lady had looked towards Mr Ransom, a silent witness to all this.

"They have also a fine house in London, cousin Robert, and Mr Fitzdowne is, I have heard, to inherit a fortune from his godmother. Which is why, no doubt, he has often been sought as a husband for daughters or sisters or nieces whose parents and guardians have high ambitions. Such young ladies, my dear cousin, you may or may not know by now, are frequently gained by the highest bidder.''

Robert stepped back a little, as if dashed by her words and the fiercely bitter tone in which they were spoken.

''Is there anything further you wish me to tell you?'' she asked coldly.

''Nay . . .'' He sounded confused.

''There is one other thing I may not have made plain. It is that rich men always cry for more riches – so it is best for them when the hand they seek holds wealth of its own.''

Robert turned on his heel as she moved away. He ran blundering into Ned and almost knocked him down.

''What are you doing? You're eavesdropping! The kitchen's your place! Get out of here before I punch your stupid head!''

5

THREE DAYS went by in a passion of preparation. It was as
well Mrs Hannah had insisted on cleaning the house right
through the very instant Sir Joshua left home. The place could
not otherwise have been anything like ready, at such short
notice, for so many visitors. Even so, the scurry was infernal,
with tempers lost and manners forgotten as they rushed up
and down the stairs, aired bed linen long in the press, washed
and flat-ironed pillowberes and healings, made up beds,
smoothed them with warming-pans, filled pitchers and set
candles and tinder-boxes at bedsides and on toilet-tables.

By midnight on that third day, the frenzy was still at its
height, while Sir Athelstan's major domo ordered and dis-
approved and cursed and demanded and generally upset
every maid about the house, every man about the yard that he
saw fit to address.

"This is not as Sir Althelstan expects," was his most
damning remark, for it seemed to set at naught everything
that Winterpicks could offer.

Only Mrs Hannah refused to be quelled by his manners,
constantly challenging his opinions, refusing his advice. Until
poor Miss Felicity was urging her to quiet, and fat Mrs
Dorothea, who would keep interfering, was reduced from
sighing to weeping, from weeping to wild sobbing and
eventually into a dead faint.

"There she lie," Lucy cried to the others, "fat as a bolster
and will not budge, but lies moaning and snoring like a badger
in its holt. Give us a handle o' they duck feathers, Mrs Betty,
and I'll burn 'em in a chafing dish – summat's got to bring her
to sense or she'll give up and die, surelye!"

Presently word reached the kitchen that the old lady had recovered just far enough to take to her bed; which at least kept her out of the way.

The excitement in the body of the house could hardly compare with the frenzy in the kitchen. Anxiety ran high, and since Mrs Betty's state of mind sent her for strength to the brandy bottle, it was felt that disaster could strike at any moment. Great joints were being cooked for cold cutting, with chickens and capons, ox-tongues and hams and innumerable sweetmeats and puddings to be laid out on the shelves of the huge cold larder. And every time Mrs Betty picked up a dish of whatever delicacy, it was expected that she would drop it on the floor.

The heat for good roasting had to be maintained. It was those who cared for the hearth and the spit, Ned Only and Turnboy, suffered the most. The spit, with its banked racks of rails, was usually turned quite satisfactorily by the rotation of one wheel. It was so devised, by some cunning engineer of past years, that a second wheel could be called into use, with two more useful rails; and so now, on Mrs Betty's very tipsy orders, both wheels were brought into use. In this way the joints and the poultry could be constantly replenished.

The fire roared in the huge chimney, mended and fed by Ned, whose face grew scarlet and singed, covered with sweat, as was his whole body. And round and round and on and on, straining under a double load, trudged Turnboy, grease-splashed and wild-eyed. Then at last he began to cough and stagger, and before Ned could help him, he dropped down and lay limp, the wheel dragging him on until the motion died away.

"Now what's to do?" cried Mrs Betty, parting with the brandy bottle in order to rush and see why the spit had come to a halt. "Up, little beast – up on your silly short legs and back to work! There's a saddle o' mutton yet to be roast!"

"Leave him!" Ned shouted. He shoved her away with all his strength, so that she staggered back and would have sat hard on the floor, if Mary had not caught her.

Ned stooped before she could recover, released Turnboy and snatched him up. He ran with him out into the air of the yard. There he pumped water and tossed it over the dog, then held some in his cupped hands and tried to get Turnboy to drink. But the best to be done was to pour the water over his lolling tongue. Ned heard himself muttering and almost sobbing – for how would life be for him if Turnboy died? He pulled off his jerkin and laid it on the ground and rested the dog there, stroking him softly as if he dared hardly touch him, as if his hand might be too heavy for Turnboy to endure.

"Dunna you die, boy!" Ned called to him. "Come on, you, and stay wi' me! Stay wi' me, do!"

Daniel came out into the yard – perhaps Mrs Betty had sent him, for he called out roughly,

"Now what's to do? Come on back, you lazy lad. The meat'll be all spilt and good for naun."

"See he don't die, Daniel!" Ned wailed. "Come on here and see he don't die!"

Daniel came at once and crouched down by Ned. When he saw poor Turnboy he gave a whistle of dismay.

"He do look poorly. What come to him, Ned?"

"Work's killed him! He can't do n'more, Dan. You tell Mrs Betty the dog died and I'll take an' hide him in the old stable."

"Wait, now," Daniel said. "Set 'un on his feet. Gently. Best for any dog to stand upright. There. Hold him so."

Ned did as Daniel told him, holding the dog so that each of his four feet just touched the ground. After a second or two he began to scrabble at the stones and lift his head. They gave him a few drops of water and the stump of his tail moved slightly. He glanced upward. His eyes had cleared a little. There seemed to be a vestige of his usual grin . . .

"Now you get back to the kitchen, Ned. I'll take an' find a place he can lie quiet. You said the old stable. That'd be where. Never a body go near, year's end to year's end. Go on, now. Tell Mrs Betty the dog died, if you must – the lie'll be forgive you. Go on – you know I'm your friend. You can trust me, can't you?"

"I can, Daniel – I can." But still he hesitated, afraid lest the dog should die the moment his back was turned, knowing well that this was how dogs that turned spits were all but bound to die.

"Get on!" Daniel cried. He carried Turnboy away.

Ned went back to the kitchen. The air had revived him as it seemed to have revived Turnboy.

"Where's the dog?" the cook demanded.

"He'll work n'more," Ned said, but not looking at her. "He get fully jawled out and he'll work n'more."

"What's that? And how'll the roasting get done? And who'll tell the master there's not meat enough? No dog! There's plenty about the farm. Fetch another! Fetch another!"

"There's none the size," Ned said. And this time he did look at her, and with so hating a glance that she blinked and tottered a step away from him as if she thought he might harm her. Then she recovered herself and all but shouted at him, "What're you at now? What are you at now, you stupid lad?"

He was busy with the spit, unlinking the chains, releasing the wheel and then coupling up again.

"What're you at?" she cried again.

"I'll be turn boy now," he said. And began hauling at the pulleys and setting the meat once more rotating.

At ten o'clock that night the work in the kitchen at Winterpicks was concluded. Too tired even to go to bed, they sat leaning their elbows on the long table and drinking the ale that Mrs Hannah had decided everyone deserved. Sent to the cellar to draw the ale, Ned had been so weary that he spilt at least a potful on the stone floor. It took him three journeys before all were served. At the head of the table, in the only seat with a back, Mr Kite professed himself satisfied with the preparations.

"My master knows only the best. But I find that you have done well enough – well enough. At Ardland Hall there would be swan and peacock to grace the board. But it shall suffice for a short stay in rural surroundings."

57

"So the stay'll be short, Mr Kite?" said Mrs Hannah.

"What should you suppose, foolish woman? He's much in demand, my master is. For interest in business and politics you wouldn't hardly find his equal. A man of action is what I'd name him." He smirked slightly, flicking a glance round the table. "Once the business here's got done with – and I'd not expect it to take long – he'll be travelling on up to London. He has a fine mansion there'd make you swoon to see."

"Oh," said Mrs Hannah, nudging Mrs Betty, who was fast falling asleep, "oh indeed. Your master has business at Winterpicks, has he? What'd that be, could I make so bold?"

"Bold is as bold seem," said Mr Kite, rather obscurely. "They'll argue the contract, see you. Haggle over the dowry."

"The dowry!" shrieked Mrs Hannah. "The *dowry*!"

"What else? My master's son – his only son and heir – shall see what he thinks of your master's niece. But we shall see. He can take his pick, can young Mr Vereker Fitzdowne; and none he's looked at has pleased him yet."

THAT NIGHT Ned lay exhausted and aching. Lonely without Turnboy's company, he could not sleep for worrying. Daniel had taken the dog to the quiet and safety of the old stables and though there had been barely time for a word, Daniel had winked at Ned and nodded hard as he sped through the kitchen on his way to one job or another.

Ned lay there pestered by thoughts of the coming visit, the rich strangers, the difference there must be about the house while they remained. Could it be true that Sir Joshua was bringing home a suitor for his ward's hand? Was it to seek such a man that he had travelled from home? What then of Mr Ransom – what of Mistress Felicity herself? Ned tossed and huffed on his bed under the table as he considered the fate of these two people, so far out of his reach, and yet suddenly a close, important part of his life. He would surely die for the lady, if it would help her in any way to be imagined. And although he might not feel a need to go to quite such extremes for Mr Ransom, it could be a near thing, should the opportunity occur . . . As always when he thought seriously about Mr Ransom, Ned then wondered about Stephen and Peg. Had they found their way safely as Mr Ransom had directed them? Were they by this time living where they had been sent, married and content? Perhaps he would never know . . .

Above him in the silent house everyone must surely be dreaming of tomorrow. Then the coaches with their outriders would come spanking down the highway and turn in at Winterpicks' gate. The lodgekeeper and the lodgekeeper's wife and the lodgekeeper's five children would stand in a row to bow and bob a respectful welcome home to the master and mistress, a humble greeting to the guests. Seconds later, Sir Joshua Bidgood would stand once more on his own territory. On the driveway, the outside servants would be waiting; on the steps Mr Kite, no doubt, would take pride of place; in the hall, Mrs Hannah would have mustered the maids, with Daniel in his footman's dark breeches. Perhaps even Ned himself might find a place. Then, as the gentlemen and their ladies stepped in from the bright sunshine, the guests would be viewed for the first time. And that would be when Mistress Felicity and Master Robert, with Mrs Dorothea fussing about them, would step forward to greet the travellers. Nice manners would call for extreme courtesy and wine would be carried from one to the other to make the welcome more sure . . .

And it was so that events unrolled themselves – except that when morning came the weather had broken and the rain was pelting down. The party was six hours delayed on the road, arriving nearer dusk than noon. By that time tempers were frayed and the welcome suffered sadly from the exhaustion of the party. As Mary carried the tray with the wine and the glasses, her hand shook so badly that she spilt a pool of red wine at Sir Joshua's very feet. His face seemed to swell – but with a mighty effort he decided on benevolence.

"Fetch a cloth, child," he said, almost sweetly.

This in its turn so unnerved poor Mary that she almost dropped the tray itself.

By the time these formalities were over, the guests shown to their quarters and their luggage unloaded and brought indoors, any glitter that the occasion might have offered had been quite dulled. Briefly, there was a silence over the house; and with it a sense of gloom; even of disaster.

THE SUPPER that followed, though it restored the appetites of the guests, and their spirits enough for laughter, did very little to raise spirits in the kitchen. For each time the maids returned with dirty dishes, or Daniel came to open more wine, there was some startling tale to tell.

"His worship's lady eats like a horse – who ever saw such? That's two carvings o' the cold beef, and a fat partridge, and slices of ham – and all that after the fish and the sauces. And still a dozen dishes ahead!"

"Stop chattering, Lucy, and get to the junkets," Mrs Hannah snapped. "And see you cut the apple pie small else it'll be gone afore its finished! Susan – set the sugared fruits on the round silver dish. Keep some back, girl – there's all us to be fed yet, and the visiting servants. No reason we shouldn't have a taste o' what we made."

"The old gentleman's enough to frit the devil," Susan said, as she fetched and arranged the sweetmeats. "He's a squint like a gargoyle and his hands shake so he spills half he eats."

"Never mind the old gentleman – what about the young?" the cook demanded. "It's him must make the difference. Is he set next to our Mistress Felicity?"

"Aye – and she never speak a word yet," Daniel told them. "Come on, Ned – help me wi' the cellar stuff. They might be heathen elephants, the way they drink."

He went ahead of Ned down the ladder into the cellar.

"Is he handsome, Dan?" Ned asked.

"Handsome enough – so long's you don't heed he squints like his father."

"Squints?" Ned cried. "Which eye?" As if it mattered.

"Both. And grows a forked tail and two horns," Daniel

assured him. "And stutters something fierce, and limps in both legs!"

Ned was appalled. "Do you speak true? Really true."

"It's worse'n that, Ned," Daniel said.

"It never could be . . ."

"It's worse because all that's just a tale I tell. Mr Fitzdowne could be a bit taller, it's true. But his face is handsome and he speak and act like a gentleman. His manner is kind and full o' courtesy – so I see well how it must go, boy. She'll have him sure as good wine's a good red – like this'n," he said, holding up a bottle. "He'll get her and we'll lose her."

"But, Dan . . . Daniel – what about Mr Ransom?"

If Daniel had not had his hands full he would surely have struck Ned.

"Get silent, you silly nidget! Things go hard enough, wi'out you bring that name in. What if it got heard? It only need a word to make a true boffle. Never speak so agen – niver. I'll take Turnboy away for ever'n an' all – if you can't hold that silly tongue."

"I'll not say such again – I never will, I swear it . . . Is he better? True?"

"Better enough to be hungry. You get and gather up some scraps off'n the dishes – there'll be plenty!"

Ned could have cried with self-reproach. Those two names could never be spoken in the same breath, for life was already working their separation. A penniless second son could be no rival for such as Mr Vereker Fitzdowne.

As they came up from the cellar they heard the voice of Mr Kite.

"A fair enough collation, goody," he was saying to Mrs Hannah. "My master sends word to the cook. The beef a shade over-roast, but all else pretty well."

Mrs Hannah and Mrs Betty, it was clear, should have simpered and curtsyed and expressed in every possible way their gratitude for this stingy compliment. But they stood side by side with folded arms and stared insolently at the insolence of Mr Kite.

"This seems a brutish neighbourhood," he remarked. "Bring more syllabub, one of you girls. The ladies like them. The gentlemen will take brandy." And he repeated as he swaggered out, "A brutish neighbourhood. I pray there be no need to dally long in such parts."

NED KNEW, almost before his eyes were open next morning, that the sun was shining. A shaft of light, narrow as a knife, struck through a chink in the shutters and pierced his eyelids. Within seconds, it had shifted. Ned rolled over and emerged yawning, remembering instantly that Daniel had said Turnboy was recovering. It was about five o'clock and the house was waking. Ned scratched his head and shook himself violently as Turnboy might. Yawning as he crossed the floor, he went and threw back the shutters.

Washed by yesterday's torrents, the countryside, too, seemed to be shaking itself. Already the yard floor had dried. Over in the byre a cowman was singing as the milk swished down. Perhaps this same contentment, this peace after storm, would creep through all the household and today there would be smiles.

Ned ran outside and up the hill towards the spring, lacking Turnboy and feeling lost without him. If indeed the dog was recovering as well as Daniel had said, he would need to be kept hidden, for to drag him back to work would surely kill him. Resting, he might regain all his strength, for he was not an old dog in years, only because of dreadful, demanding service.

After the rain, the spring was full of sparkle. Ned dallied there, splashing more water into his face, drinking yet again from his cupped hands; he seemed to drink in the whole morning as he did so.

Then it was time to go. He ran off reluctantly towards the manor. He would take the back track and snatch time to look at Turnboy. But at the stile, someone sprang out with such a shout that he all but turned and fled.

"Out of doors!" Robert yelled.

Ned snatched back his nerve and answered firmly,

"Aye – out o'doors it is."

Robert held out his left hand. "We have always to shake hands on the bargain. Always left hand. Shake the right and that means full friends – not just out of door friends. That's what we are, so make no mistake. Out of door friends."

Ned grinned slightly, and more to himself than Robert. He felt twice as bold as at their last meeting. Robert did not see fit to smile, but there was very little in his face of the bullying and domineering that Ned was accustomed to.

"Where's the dog, Neddy?"

"He took sick."

"Did he die?"

Ned said carefully, "Not fully."

"What's that mean? You die or you don't die. So – which?"

"More work'n he'll die dead. Never tell any – shall you, friend – that Turnboy's alive? Come a month or two, Daniel tell me, he'll be well again."

Robert frowned. "Who'll turn the spit?"

"I shall."

"Then you'll die," said Robert in a flat, cross voice – as though Ned was quite clearly planning to spoil the friendship.

"Time I go," Ned said – and ran off down the hill, with Robert soon puffing alongside.

"Not so fast, you donkey!"

"They'll ask where I'm gone."

"You get on, then. I've a stitch."

"Too fat!" cried Ned – then bolted out of the way. "Out o' doors!" he yelled as he vanished from Robert's sight.

Daniel was crossing the yard. He was hurrying, but took time to nod and smile and jerk his head towards the far stable. Turnboy was better! Rejoicing was touched with worry, even with fear. To keep Turnboy safe he must do everything the dog was needed for and more. Perhaps, if he worked hard enough, they would forget in the kitchen that there had ever been a dog to turn the spit. "It is far better now," they must say. "The roast is far better with a boy turning the spit.

Whoever thought a dog could be as good?" The fact that Sir Joshua was to be much too busy with his guests to make his customary inspections of the kitchen quarters added greatly to Ned's chances of success. All the same, there must be a thousand things easier to keep hidden than a dog . . .

EACH MORNING, now, when Ned ran to the spring, Robert was ahead of him. He was so bursting with stories about the guests that Ned could hardly tear himself away and get to work.

"It's Lady Fitzdowne that's the worst – she never stops stuffing herself with sweets and comfits. She'll be twice the size of my cousin's Aunt Dorothea before she quits Winterpicks. As for Sir Athelstan, he beats all at chess save Mr Ransom. My father must pay up every time. You should see the guineas roll!"

"Is it truth," Ned asked, bolder every day, "that the young gentleman would wed wi' Mistress Felicity?"

"Of course it's true! Of course he would! What young gentleman wouldn't? He'll be rich beyond dreams when his father dies, and so's she rich, and so it goes well for my father because he's her guardian. And when the old man dies, then Mr Fitzdowne shall be Sir Vereker Fitzdowne and my cousin his Lady. And curses on it, I say," Robert ground out in a great rage, "that my father is none better than a knight, and so I must be plain Mister. Who'll I get to wed with me but some silly miss of no importance!"

Ned had nothing to say to all that. Robert's marriage seemed a long way ahead and so there was little need to be angry over the importance or otherwise of his bride. Besides, he was more concerned for the matters in hand. Robert spoke as though all was settled and his cousin as near betrothed as made no matter.

"Shall she have him, then? Shall she so?"

"My father'll see to it. Mark that for sure, Ned Only. My father will make certain she does what he says."

Now Ned hesitated, eyeing Robert doubtfully. He thought

of Stephen and Peggy and that look in Stephen's eyes. Out of some distant memory of home he recalled his father seizing his wife round the waist and swinging her up and kissing her, and how she had flung her arms round his neck and kissed him, too. It was a picture printed on the eager memory of a young child, the only happy picture – and it would never fade.

"But do she *fancy* him?" he insisted, frowning and anxious.

Robert was leaning against a tree-trunk, his hands thrust into his breeches pockets. He gave a great sigh, biting his lip and staring at the ground. He looked then so unlike his more usual, bullying self, that Ned almost felt Sir Joshua must have two sons, one in the house and one out of it . . . The outdoor Robert gloomily shook his head.

"Never. She never could."

Ned forgot Daniel's warning. The words burst from him, a cry of actual pain –

"Then what of Mr Ransom?"

Robert's expression changed instantly. He flung himself at Ned and bowled him over, then sat on his chest and seized him by the ears.

"Never speak his name! My father would starve her and beat her if he thought she so much as smiled at him! Swear not to name him! Swear it, you donkey – you stupid Neddy, you!"

"I do – I do swear!" A word came to Ned from their first encounter, up in the wood. "Pax!" he bellowed.

Robert let him go. When they finally reached the house, as if to remind them both of the terms of their agreement, he gave him a kick indoors, hissing as he did so, "See you do as I bid! See you keep faith, you greasy turnspit!"

AT THE END of two weeks, the guests were still installed at Winterpicks. What had seemed strange and exhausting became a matter of routine. It was as though there had always been seven gentry to cater for, always so many dishes to wash, so many beds to make, such quantities of laundry – shirts and caps and bonnets and ribbons and chemises and petticoats, stockings of all sizes. Had there ever been fewer gentlemen's boots to shine, ladies' slippers to brush and polish, water to carry, slops to empty? The servants at Winterpicks began to wonder what they had found to do while only the family was at home.

In the kitchen and closet there were various trials of a less practical nature. Mr Kite expected any girl to offer him favours, Minette quarrelled with the visiting ladies' maid, Henry accused Sir Athelstan's valet of cheating at cards. The only harmony seemed to be between the incoming coachman and the resident coachman, the two grooms and Sir Joshua's grooms. It was easier to be friendly, it appeared, in quarters away from the manor house.

And then, without any previous hint, without warning of what was to come, the climax of the visit was announced: On the night of the full moon, a mere ten days ahead, Sir Joshua and Lady Bidgood would give a ball in honour of the guests.

6

Now so much had to be prepared that men were brought from the nearby village to swell the staff, along with a farmer's three daughters. All these felt themselves higher in the world than the rest. It was well known that Sir Joshua's servants were all unfortunate dependants living on his charity, and they were properly despised for it. The Winterpicks people closed ranks, as in the face of an enemy. They worked as never in their lives before, all petty rivalries and personal squabbles forgotten.

Dressmakers arrived from the town with boxes and bales of silks to make ballgowns for the ladies. Invitations were drawn up by Sir Joshua, inscribed by Mr Ransom and despatched about the county; Daniel was courier. The upheaval could hardly have been greater if the King himself had been coming to honour the occasion, or so Mrs Hannah concluded.

"And for why's the rumpus?" she demanded. "To point the way to a wedding, if I was asked. You'll see. They'll cry the betrothal after suppertime."

During all the flurry Ned was kept so busy at his own tasks that he barely caught sight of the gentry except for Robert. Once, it was true, he had seen the young lady walking down the avenue before supper time, and Mr Fitzdowne with her. When she turned her head away, Ned was just able to see how pale she looked, and her movements were stiff and without their usual grace.

But the two boys met most mornings by the spring. Daniel still kept Turnboy safely, but nearly always Ned took a roundabout way to the spring, collecting the dog on his way, but well out of sight of the house. Robert kept his word to his

67

out-of-door friend, pretending that this was some quite different dog, giving Turnboy other names – like Ratter and Scrumper, Hunty and Bravo. But through all these more cheerful matters ran the threat of disaster that both boys feared so intensely. Names were not named, except in a stealthy, sideways fashion, as – "Does the lady smile?" "She hardly speaks." "Will it be told at the ball?" "Ask my father," said Robert, growling it, his face red and yet somehow thin with anxiety – which made him look a different person.

"Ah, but she never'll say Yes," Ned insisted, again and again.

And like some weary old man, Robert would reply,

"It's money says *Yes* in the end."

NED WAS IN the yard, filling buckets at the pump. The whole floor of the hall was to be first scrubbed, then washed with milk, then done over with beeswax and turpentine; for here they would dance at the ball, now less than a week ahead. There would be a harp and two fiddles to make the music; Mr Ransom had been sent riding to the town in search of musicians. When he returned with news of the arrangements he had been able to make, Sir Joshua promptly complained that they were demanding twice as much as they were worth. It was Lucy who reported this. She had been holding pins for the dressmaker and had returned to the kitchen by the back stairs just as Sir Joshua was pacing the parlour and making a great bellow about it all.

"What, then?" cried Susan and Mary.

"Well, sir, says Mr Ransom," Lucy told them between giggles, "we cannot tell their worth, sir, he says, till we have sampled their skills ... Or some such high-sounding words."

Mrs Hannah had laughed loudly and harshly at Lucy's tale, and had even, Ned remembered with some alarm, muttered something about 'the old fool'. Just as Mr Ransom's sympathetic manner had seemed to give them all some heart, so now their feelings rose to the plight of their young lady, the helpless victim of her guardian's greed. Sir Athelstan, too, to judge by the time affairs were taking, was so much the better bargainer that Sir Joshua was beginning to appear in the eyes of his servants as even smaller than his height and girth allowed . . .

Ned had humped two of the buckets indoors and returned for the second pair, when he saw Robert beckoning from the yard gate. Ned looked round him uneasily, for there was such coming and going at the present that he seemed to find someone at his elbow every minute of the day. But now the yard was empty, so he went across to the gate and they exchanged the required greeting.

"Mr Ransom's too busy for lessons. Come on, Neddy – play truant."

"Nay, I never could," Ned replied at once, frowning. "There's work – a mortacious great lot."

"Come on, stupid, come while there's none about to stop you. I'll take the blame, if I must. I've got the pony saddled and waiting. We can ride turns to the top of the downs."

"I'd be sore punished . . ."

"Come *on*! Coward Neddy!"

Ned saw his supper disappearing, at the very least; but the thought of gaining the summit that had so long teased him was hard to resist.

"Wait and I'll hump the buckets."

Robert heaved his bulky self over the wall. "You take two, I'll take two."

"Stay where you stand!" Ned cried, shocked to imagine the master's son so free with his labour. "My work's my work, and lessons is yourn."

He made the two journeys as fast as the weight and the slopping allowed. He glanced at the row standing under the window – six brim-full loads. Water goes a long way, he remembered, once it has escaped. He easily persuaded himself that more could not possibly be needed, while as for spit-turning, there could be none required for at least a couple of hours. That seemed a long time and he did not pause to measure the possible distance. He ran to join Robert and they dashed off.

"Fetch old Scrumper, Ned."

"Too long a way for'm yet."

"Whoso's on the pony can carry him, if he tires."

With every second, the expedition increased in charm for Ned.

"I'll meet you t'other side the byre," he said.

It was an easy day for getting over the ground. There had been no rain to speak of for almost a week and the ancient grassy track, laid long ago on flinty ground, was dry and surprisingly level. In the way of sick animals who have seemed near to death, Turnboy had recovered his spirits magnificently, and raced and bounded almost as never before.

"The rest did him good, Neddy."

"But we'll not over-do 'un?"

"No, stupid Neddy, we never shall! Get your silly self out of my way – I'm going to gallop Jenny the next mile."

He was off. The sunshine was very faintly misted and in no time he and Jenny had almost vanished against the grassy background. Robert rode boldly but not beautifully; his size was bound to make him a bit sack-like, Ned thought. Somehow he was pleased with himself for thinking so. Even as the distance between them lengthened, Ned still heard Robert's shouts of pleasure, his urging on of the pony, keen enough, but a little fat, like her rider.

Now Turnboy was tearing ahead while Ned ran after, puffing in no time and having to hold his side. For a moment he wondered if Robert had tricked him, had urged him along and then abandoned him . . . But he was waiting among a clump of alder that was rooted along the rim of a small pond.

He slid out of the saddle. "Come on, you. Turn and turn about – remember? I'll give you a leg up. Never fear – Jenny's too puffed to bolt with you. Come on, cowardy – did you never have your leg over a pony's back till now?"

"I never did. How should I?" He stepped back. "Best stick

to your nag, Master Robert, sir. I know better'n you how to use my own legs."

He ducked and side-stepped, for he thought Robert was going to knock him down. His face looked as it had done when he played the fool with the log basket. He turned very red, but there was more to it than anger. He was his cousin's *monster*, but he was also Mr Ransom's *lonely boy*. He ground his teeth together in a fury, but there were tears in his eyes.

"Out of doors!" he shouted, his voice breaking and squeaking. "Out of doors, you lout – you silly slave!"

The word did not mean much to Ned. Once he had stood at the back of the church with the farm people and heard Mr Langridge preach a sermon and there had been slaves in that – we are slaves of wickedness, he had said, slaves of base nature .. Or some such words ... He moved to the pony, saying, "Joss me up, then."

In silence, Robert gave him a leg into the saddle. Ned felt himself to be hoisted so high above the world that he was a king. Instinctively he gripped the pony between his knees and almost put her into a canter. It was good that he did so, for it made Robert laugh. It was a huge, mocking laugh, convulsing him as he grabbed the bridle and hung on, helping him back to friendliness. In a way, Ned understood. He joined in gladly.

"Old Runty looks a mite weary," Robert said, picking up Turnboy. "Take him up with you and I'll lead Jenny. That way you and he can rest – and so shall the pony."

It solved everything. Dignity was restored, nervousness banished. They moved in harmony through the sunny morning, mounting all the while to the green skyline from which they would surely look on wonders. Time passed without notice; larks rose and descended; thyme patched the turf; there had been nothing like it in Ned's lifetime and perhaps not in Robert's. That Ned might be punished, might catch a beating or a box of the ear, was now not merely unimportant – the possibility had gone from his mind.

Turn and turn about, they mounted on a now winding

chalky track to the last layer of the downs and so came to the extreme summit and stared about them.

IT WAS THE TOP of the world. Robert took Turnboy and set him down, while Ned slid from the saddle. Turnboy ran and raced. The pony began at once to crop the grass, shaved by the winds into turf pricked out with low growing herbs – harebells and tufting thrift and daisies. When they turned northward there was nothing to break the horizon's rim, but from the east the green merged into blue. The sea, as Daniel had once promised, completed the circle to westward.

Robert shouted and flung himself down, grabbing at Turnboy, hugging him and roughing the hair between his ears, rolling over and over on the grass, the excited dog leaping at him and about him.

Ned stared, amazed, at the sea. It looked firm enough to walk on, smiling, without treachery. From some shore village fishing boats were out, rocking at anchor. Then, as one hauled in its net, a great cloud of sea birds came from nowhere to swoop and dip and circle in a shrieking mob. If Ned had ever dreamt quite clearly of standing here, all would have been just so. He dropped on to his haunches and gazed. Turnboy abandoned Robert and ran to the one he knew best in his life. The dog's tongue lolled from a wide grinning mouth.

"I said you should come with me," Robert cried, "and I was right."

Ned, not yet ready to talk, mumbled in reply.

"If we went on and on, Ned, we'd come right down the hillside to the sea. I never was there, but I've heard enough. There's great cliffs, white almost, and sand. Or maybe the cliffs are in another part and here it's just sand. Mr Ransom knows about it. Seaweed, he says, that grows under the waves and gets left by the tide. Shiny wet. And over the sand, Mr Ransom says, the tide comes in so shallow you can see shrimps and crabs scuttling – very small ones, he said, that don't know enough yet to get away faster!"

The mention of Mr Ransom was enough to bring Ned back

from wherever he had been dallying – in some strange corner of his own mind that he had not explored before, where he found with astonishment that life was not all a manor house kitchen.

Robert moved to squat down beside Ned.

"Mr Ransom," he said. "There's no better gentleman, even though he came to work at Winterpicks for a living. I wish he'd carry off my cousin. I'd help them. I would. I'd help them get away. Would you?" He looked quickly sideways at Ned and then frowned. "You've turned pale as linen. You'd be afraid!"

"The master'd be after wi' horsemen and clubs . . . "

"That's why I'd help, you ninny!" Robert almost shouted it. "But would *you*? Two's better than one. Answer! Answer!"

A sudden piercing shrewdness, stronger than all else he was feeling at that strange moment, showed Ned his advantage. Robert was beseeching him. Robert was at his mercy, amazing as that seemed. There could be a bargain . . . It seemed to take him a long time to reach this point, but Robert still waited, so maybe it was no more than a second.

He said boldly, "We'd need be indoor friends, then. Outdoor's not enough . . . "

Then, even before Robert could answer, Ned was distracted. He cried out in alarm,

"What come to Turnboy? Quick! Look at'm!"

The dog was standing alert, ears pricked, nose up, his whole body quivering.

"A rabbit?"

"No . . . No – othersome . . . "

The dog ran forward, then checked, paw lifted, nose pointing now. Then he dropped and lay with his nose between his paws, but still quivering from whiskers to tail tip.

"What trouble you, boy?" Ned cried. He crouched down and tried to take the dog in his arms, but Turnboy leapt away and again ran forward, again stood taut and trembling, staring into the distance, staring inland, pricking his ears.

Over all the countryside there seemed no change of light or

sound. The summer noon dazzled over the warm ground. Somewhere sheep were bleating – was that what Turnboy heard, had suddenly become aware of? He surely could not be listening to birdsong, and the sea birds' crying over the fishermen's catch was done now.

Then Robert said, "What's that?"

"What? Where?"

"Quiet, can't you . . . Listen!"

"There's naun . . ."

"There is, then. I can hear it. So can Turnboy."

Then Ned heard it, too. A thin thread of sound that might be an insect close at hand or a great crowd far away. Continuous and unwavering at first, but increasing soon, becoming very gradually no whine, no hum but a growing clamour, now of beasts lowing, then of men calling, but all so far, so very far away.

"What is it?" Ned asked, almost in a whisper, feeling the strangeness of it in the very roots of his hair.

"Look out!" Robert shouted. "Catch him! Hold him!"

Ned lunged after Turnboy and fell flat as he grabbed him. The dog yelped and struggled, his claws scoring Ned's arms and once even his face. Ned held on till the dog was quiet, though he panted, still, and whined.

Meanwhile the sound was increasing, and soon they saw on a fold of downland, a spur of the long coastal spine that leant and reached from west to east, some movement against the sky.

Along the horizon and spilling over the slopes there moved a great concourse of men and beasts, cattle being driven, men alongside, behind and before, constantly shifting to prevent straying, herding and driving purposefully towards some far destination. Then among the crowd it was possible to see some riders, and, lower to the ground like a second wave taking its own course, some smaller beast which even at this distance could be seen to move in a blundering rhythmless way.

"Geese," Robert said, as though he had solved the problem. "Geese, Ned! You know what that means?"

"How'd I know? What is it? What's to happen?"

"It's the drovers, Ned! The drovers!"

"The drovers! Them's Turnboy's own people – didn' Dan say it long ago? Mind and hold him fast! Otherly, we'll lose 'un!"

Between them they were all but throttling the poor dog, as he struggled ever harder. The sound swelled of beasts and men. Every now and again there came a strange, unintelligible shout, as the drovers strove to keep their herds steady and straight on the hill track that must run for miles and miles into distance and silence. The curve of the downland gradually received men and beasts and birds. They poured over the brow and began to disappear, as if into some great maw, some chasm that consumed them by tens and twenties. And then, as if indeed they waged a struggle against annihilation, their cries grew fainter and then ceased. The quiet slid back like a shutter.

Now Turnboy lay unmoving, but whimpering quietly, as if he had been held back from heaven. Ned pressed his face down by the dog's muzzle. His own eyes were full of tears for some opportunity missed, some chance let go that surely would never come again.

"Wake up, old donkey," Robert said.

"I'm not sleeping."

"What then?"

Ned was afraid to look up in case some tears had actually escaped to his cheeks – for how would his out of door friend receive that?

"Did you see 'm ever before?"

"The drovers? Once. Not so many as that, though. It was the time they brought cattle to the High Sheriff. They go most to London markets, I'd say. There's plague in London. Maybe that's why they're driving further south."

"Daniel was right, weren't he? A drover's dog, he said. Turnboy's a drover's dog. I'n't he?"

"Perhaps any dog'd want to run off with them?"

"He heard 'em – before any. He'd've gone. I'd've lost 'un. He knew what he heard."

"He did want to run to them," Robert agreed. "Maybe the time he got lost was when they came with the High Sheriff's cattle. When exactly did Turnboy come, Ned? When was he found in the yard?"

But Ned could not remember how long he and Turnboy had shared the pile of sacks under the kitchen table. He had not been much inclined to thinking then.

"When?" Robert insisted.

"I misremember." He looked sideways and briefly at Robert's face that had once seemed so fat and bullying, and now seemed fat enough, certainly, but friendly. "Shall they come agin – ever?"

"My father once said he'd send to buy some of the Welsh cattle for himself."

"Will he, then? When will he? Shall you tell'm we saw the drovers? That'd remember him."

"It's no good talking to him now. He's all for dancing and new clothes and breeches with ribbons."

"Another day, then . . ."

"Maybe," said Robert. He looked the least bit suspiciously at Ned but said no more.

Now the bright noon was given back to the larks and the distant sheep. The pony munched again, then shook her head against the flies, so that the bit jingled. All was as it had been before the drovers passed on the far downland, yet for Ned all was changed. He yearned after the drovers, for the freedom of days in the open, Turnboy with him, driving the beasts all across England; from Wales, that he could not imagine, to London, which, plague or not, was the only city name he knew . . .

"Wake up," Robert said. "You never answered my question – that I asked before the drovers came."

"Nor you never answered mine," Ned said.

"Come on then, Ned," said Robert, "let it be full friends, indoors and out. I promise." He looked suddenly, astonishingly anxious. "You promise, too, then – you give your word . . ."

"Aye." The word just came out audibly.

"I'll swear, if you like."

Ned remained speechless. He nodded. He had never had occasion or opportunity to imagine a friend of his own age – and certainly not his master's only son, disliked by all the servants and called by his own cousin "a monster".

"Then shall you do as I asked first," Robert persisted, having accepted that nod as promise enough. "I mean – to help if need be? You know what I am talking about."

Ned frowned, uncertain whether he most wanted Mr Ransom to be bold, or to remain honourable and gentlemanly. His final nod was reluctant.

Robert gave a sigh that must be of relief and cried with sudden vigour, "There, then – that's settled. Now we'll go on to the sea."

"Now?" Ned was startled, his mouth almost as wide as his eyes.

"When shall we be so far on the way again?"

Ned sprang up, calling to Turnboy, reckless and daring. He ran off fast down the narrow track, not much better than a rabbit run, that seemed to point the way.

"Wait!" yelled Robert, dashing to catch up the pony's bridle and tug her with him.

But Ned jogged on, oblivious to everything but now, when the heat hung over the chalky sides of the downs and insects hovered and hummed. Now the larks were silent and the sheep forgotten. A hawk drifted, then swooped. After that, all was still, an increasing haze blurring the distance. As they descended the hillside, so the sea vanished from their sight. The pony moved slower and slower in the heat and so did the boys, so did the dog.

They began to idle, content with what they had, knowing their purpose but losing it, almost forgetting where they were going, hardly speaking. Ned whistled, but without any tune, since he knew none. Then he stopped whistling in surprise, for Robert had begun to sing. His high treble came strangely from his sturdy body, and made Ned grin the more when it cracked and wavered. The singer seemed not the least bashful.

"We should've brought our catapults," he said, when the song was over.

"Why'd we need 'em?"

"To get a rabbit. We'd make a fire and set about roasting. We'd have stayed till dark. Longer. Through moonlight. Watched the sun come up over the ocean . . ."

Ned stopped dead, chilled by recollection.

"Late," he said. "It's late!"

He glanced up at the sky and saw how far the sun was declining. The whole day was passing, and it was passing, too, in the manor kitchen. They would have been shouting for him, searching. He heard in imagination Mrs Betty's screeching cries, Mrs Hannah's robuster raging. And what then? What would have happened then? What cries of fury and abuse were waiting, what punishments?

Ned turned and ran, Turnboy following. Robert shouted after him, but he would not even hear. The downside was steep, slippery after days of sunshine and he panted up it, climbing rather than walking. They had come a very long way and he dared not attempt any short cut. He must get to the summit before he could tell the way they had come that morning. Then he did indeed get to the top and the long track ahead was worse than he could remember.

Robert rode up, the pony snorting.

"Ned! Ride her home! You ride her, Ned . . ."

"I can't! I can't! I never sat a pony not to ride proper. Let be – I mun go fast!"

At that Robert pulled back and let him go. He did not overtake Ned again, and Ned was glad of it. By now he was sobbing a bit as he ran, catching his breath, often stumbling, tripping – once falling flat. A sharp stitch in his side stopped him in his tracks and for a bit he dared not run. By the time he saw Winterpicks lying ahead and below, the sunlight had taken a darker tinge, the mist receded. Shadows grew momently longer. He would not go to the kitchen without seeing Turnboy safe, so he staggered round past the byres to the old stable that was the dog's quarters.

Robert was there ahead of him, dismounted and waiting.

"Give me the dog. I'll see him safe – get him fresh water. He doesn't look too bad, after all. Dogs are clever." Then he caught at Ned's arm. "My fault, old donkey."

Ned pulled away. He ran back and crossed the yard and shoved through into the kitchen.

It was quiet. They were all there, standing about, as if waiting for him.

Then he understood.

Sir Joshua had come to the kitchen to inspect.

7

NED FROZE ON the threshold. He saw them all lined up, as they always lined up when Sir Joshua came to the kitchen. Then, as Ned stopped dead at the door, everyone swung round to gaze at him, the girls round-eyed, Daniel expressionless, Mrs Betty with a hand clapped over her mouth, Mrs Hannah...? Mrs Hannah had somehow not quite the look that Ned would have expected.

Sir Joshua was seated as usual on his stool. He did not move but called sharply as he might to a dog.

"Here, boy!"

Ned dared not put one foot in front of the other. Mrs Hannah spoke, most unexpectedly, and his gaze swung to her in astonishment and relief – for her tone was quite soft.

"Come now, Ned – the master must speak wi' you."

She moved across to him and took his arm, urging him forward, yet not fiercely, only firmly. For the first time since he had been taken in to the Winterpicks kitchen Ned found that the housekeeper was his ally. She had changed, she had shifted ground; she was with him against Sir Joshua. Ned's fear, though it did not leave him, instantly lessened. He stood before Sir Joshua and he was not alone. Mrs Hannah remained only a pace or two away.

Sneaking a quick glance round him at the rest, Ned saw that the whole picture of the kitchen, so familiar and, at these moments, alarming, had changed. In the past when Sir Joshua teased and taunted Ned Only, the rest had more than half enjoyed watching, thanking their stars that they were not the victims. Now in their wide-eyed watching there was sympathy for Ned and resentment towards Sir Joshua. What was it that had happened since last Sir Joshua made one of his kitchen visits? Ned knew in his heart, though he could not put it quite straight in his troubled mind. Mr Ransom had happened. Because of him, because of his manner, his sympathy, because of words casually yet sincerely spoken, they all knew that there could be more to a master than bullying and cruelty. Mr Ransom, seemingly so far above them, so gentlemanly in manner and appearance, had yet made it clear that he, too, was a servant, one of them, a part of their company. He had given them back some of their pride, so nearly bullied right out of them. It was this pride that now rallied in support of Ned and against the master . . .

"Speak up, speak up, you young wretch!" Sir Joshua cried, unaware of these mysterious changes, and banging as usual with his cane on the stone floor. "Where've you been? How dared you go? What d'you suppose should be done with you? How shall you be punished? Speak up!"

"I beg your pardon, sir," Ned replied, more dignified than would have seemed possible a moment or two earlier.

"Why, you young devil – who are you to beg my pardon? A gentleman may beg my pardon, not a miserable charity lad. *Where've you been?*"

Where had he been? Almost to heaven, Ned might have said, the fine hot day, the downs, the sea, the drovers, all floating in a gilded pattern through his memory. He almost smiled.

"Tell the master where you bin, Ned," said Mrs Hannah, sounding now a little sharper, but still a shadow of her usual self.

"A long way . . . " he began.

Then he broke off. And now he did smile, for someone had come into the kitchen and Sir Joshua's eyes almost burst from their sockets at the sight of him.

"And what are you doing here, sir? And for that matter, where have you been hiding yourself all this long day – absent from your studies – wasting your tutor's time that I must pay for?"

Robert said in a rather loud voice, "I took Ned to look at the sea."

It sounded so absurd that Lucy laughed outright, and Sir Joshua was far too concerned with his own feelings even to glare at her.

"To look at the sea? What does that mean?"

"I rode out Jenny. Ned came for company – I asked him – I told him to come with me. We went to the top of the downs and then, on a sudden, it was late. So Ned ran home in a fuss. The fault," said Robert, loud again, "was altogether mine."

He looked at Ned as he spoke, and there was something in the tilt of his chin that suggested great self-satisfaction. Now indeed he was being a friend indoors as well as out and this simple fact seemed for a second or two to leave his father speechless. His cane tapped furiously, his hands almost trembled. It was as though his mouth were stuffed with words but none would do his bidding. When at last his voice burst its way through, it came in almost a squeak, so that he was obliged to stop and swallow and start again.

"Do you know what you have done, Master Robert Bidgood? You, the only son of the house, heir to all I possess, have taken away the kitchen boy on that day of all days when he is most needed! Do you not understand that in this house are important guests? That I am lavishing my hospitality for their sake? And that, knowing all this, you *removed the turnspit* from his place in the kitchen?"

"I beg your pardon," said Robert, and there was a yawn in his voice.

"Am I to insult our guests with a lack of good roast meat for the feasting? Am I to be humiliated in their eyes – because my son, riding his pony, sought the low company of the kitchen boy? Upon my word, sir, you shall be thrashed for this and miss all the dancing! Go to your room, sir, and wait there for what shall most certainly come upon you. Mr Ransom shall be sent to deal with you ... Go! Go! And as for the stupid boy," he continued, when Robert had left the room, "the stupid boy who so presumed to go along with my son – let Jem the waggoner deal with him!"

"Then what of the spit-turning, master?" cried Mrs Hannah, quick and sharp. "The dog's went and died, there's none other but the boy can turn, for the girls fall faint at the heat. There's still the roasting – and I'll not answer for what come to they great joints should you see fit to drag in one of the farm lads . . . No indeed, sir, it may seem easy to you, sir, a small matter, sir – but what'll his worship and his lady think to this household if the meat come tough and the poultry bloody?"

"Enough!" shouted Sir Joshua. "I'll stay here no longer if I must bandy words with a pack of numbskulls. Do what you will, but see there's no single item to cause any guest a raised eyebrow. For, be sure of this, if it were so there'd be a high price to pay – a high price indeed!"

He was on his feet, his face red, his eyes starting – then he was gone, the door, shoved hard behind him, slamming with such violence that the hams smoking among the rafters swung on their hooks like bell-clappers.

"He'll have the house broke down," said Daniel; and at the sound of his voice the bemusement that had held them like some terrible magician's spell shattered and was gone. They burst out into gabbling and giggling and cries of hysterical relief.

Mrs Hannah was looking thoughtfully at Ned.

"We'll need find you clean breeches and a seemly jerkin," she said. "On the night of the ball every man and boy's to carry torches to light the guests up the avenue." She looked him up and down as if measuring him, but less for his size than for a sudden importance she might find in him. "Seems you come own servant to Master Robert. Well now, I'd say that call for a cleaning up. And one o' the girls best take the shears to that hair o' yourn . . . Now get to your work, you idle lout," she added, but still with a new tone in her voice. "Get on! Get on or it'll be the worse!"

Amazed almost out of his wits by all this, Ned stood gaping and staring like an owl.

"Get about it!" Mrs Hannah roared, in a more familiar tone. "It'll be work till midnight and on, and none to blame but your silly self!"

She gave him a great shove that sent him flying. He all but tripped and fell full length across the hearth. That was more like old times . . . All the same, Ned knew that Jem's strong arm was not to be called for; he knew that he had somehow risen in the world, that his life had taken a sudden turn. What he could not begin to imagine was where it might lead.

TURNBOY stirred in the straw at Ned's side and Ned was instantly awake; he had joined Turnboy in the stable as the weather grew hot. The half-door was open to the morning, already warm, the sun hazed over. Robert was peering in.

"It's daylight! Rouse up, you sluggard, you. I'll race you to the spring."

Thus, each of the three days since the day they played truant, Robert Bidgood came to wake Ned and run with him through a morning still dawn-coloured. The moment he saw that Ned had opened his eyes, Robert was off, needing the advantage over the fleeter, lighter boy. Each day the weather had been hot and heavy from the start, later turning thundery. Ned, too, was panting by the time he reached the spring. Work had been endless since that evening when Sir Joshua visited the kitchen. The heat of the fire, the smell of the roasting, the sheer flurry and urgency of the preparations for the great ball had exhausted every one of them.

"I'm tired, too, I can tell you," Robert said, shaking the water from his face and hair – for these days what Ned did Robert must also do. "Everyone's tired. Wherever shall come the strength for dancing and such?" He glanced over his cupped hands at Ned, saying between gulps of water, "You look to me what *you'd* call fair jawled out."

"Jawled out I am, and soon be worse, I daresay." He dashed the water over his head in the manner Robert liked to copy, and rubbed hard at his hair till it stood like a hedgehog's spines. "Shall Mr Ransom be in the dancing?"

84

"How should I know. My father never said – and why should he?"

"If be," Ned persisted, "shall he step out with Mistress Felicity?"

"I can't tell that, either, donkey. It's certain he'd wish to."

They had both escaped a beating after their truancy – Ned was needed so much in the kitchen that no further word of punishment had been spoken, while Robert had escaped with a talking-to from his tutor. Mr Ransom had seemed more intent, so Robert said, on where they had been, what they had seen on the way . . .

"Mrs Hannah find me good dark breeches," Ned said now. "An' a jerkin only needed a mite o' stitching. Lucy done that." He grinned at Robert and said in a sly way, "Shall you think to know me still, Master Robert, when I'm stood wi' a torch by the roadway, and you step forth to give the gentry greeting?"

Robert escaped answering by shoving Ned back against the rock where the water fell, and setting about him with doubled fists and bellows of mock fury. This made Turnboy growl and then break into angry barking; he danced at Robert's heels, ready to snap and hang on.

"Some'un'll hear!" Ned cried. "Let be, you grummert! Some'un'll find he's not dead!"

"Hush, you," Robert said, stooping at once to quiet the dog with caresses. "Never fear, Ned Only – I'll care for him as well as you can."

They went back, then, Robert, by their present custom, returning the dog to the stable and making him safe, Ned hurrying straight to work.

Mr Kite was in the kitchen, but dressed for travel.

"Then shall you not stay till the ball be done?" Mrs Hannah was asking.

"Heaven forbid. There's little more tedious, should you ask me, than the grand folks at their junketing. I've seen a deal too many such matters in my day. It's hard to choose, at such great affairs, which acts the sillier – the ladies or the gentlemen. I've better things to do than stay staring at 'em . . .

And now, Mrs Hannah, I'm to be off and see Ardland Court in good order for my master's return."

"So he'll leave at last, then," Mrs Hannah said.

"He would ordinarily be proceeding to London – but the plaguy plague sends gentlefolk to their country places."

"Well, once they're away, Mr Kite, I don't mind saying a bit o' peace to this household shall be very welcome."

"I doubt you've seen the last of the family," Mr Kite said, smiling his loftiest smile. "Well, well, I'd best ready myself. The devil's in it, but I'm first to ride the old dame back home – ten mile in the wrong direction, so to hell with her."

He meant Mrs Dorothea. Having served her purpose while the family was away, she had stayed on, day by day, hoping Lucy said, to be present at the ball. But there would be over-night guests and her room would be needed, so off the poor soul must go. And so, an hour later in spite of all urgings to haste, she was hauled up to ride pillion behind Mr Kite – which he declared must kill his horse. They went off down the avenue, the old lady in floods of tears, with Miss Felicity running alongside and calling out words of comfort. Ned was brushing the steps and watched it all.

He was still slowly shoving the broom back and fore when the young lady returned to the house. She looked pale and walked slowly, her eyes downcast. She would be too much in her thoughts, surely, to notice him. . . ?

But when she saw him her expression lightened and she spoke to him at once.

"I have asked Mrs Hannah to lend me your services this morning, Ned. The roasting's over now, she tells me. We must cut flowers and green boughs to deck the house. Shall you be sorry to help me?"

He shook his head, speechless with pleasure.

"Then see you bring me baskets and shears," she ordered him, "and a barrow to carry all easily. I shall look for you here in an hour's time."

She went on into the house, and he was left to wonder how he would measure the hour.

Helping the lady pick flowers was even more of an enjoyment than Ned had imagined possible. For a start, though two gardeners came with them and cut as she instructed, all that was cut was handed to Ned to put in the barrow. Even he was aware that he was not really necessary to the undertaking, and the gardeners let him know it, too. Every time they cut they tried to get to the barrow before him, so that Ned was left looking idle and foolish. But she addressed herself almost entirely to Ned. "Which shall it be?" she would ask him. "The red? The pink? Shall we take the low branch – or the high? Give him the blue flowers," she then ordered the gardener who had been cutting spires of that aconite called 'monkshood', "He handles them well and gently."

And so over half the morning went by, till at last the gardeners were dismissed, but Ned was called back.

"When you have had your dinner," she said, "come to the hall. We'll see how best to fill the vases. Be sure to return. Tell Mrs Hannah I need you."

All this was as bewildering as it was flattering. He wished he might speak of it to Robert, but Robert did not appear. The tailor was in the house with the finished garments for tomorrow; Robert must have his fine new suit fitted and tried, with perhaps a stitch or two to be added. All over the house this was happening, for even Sir Athelstan had ordered new clothes for the occasion; and since he would trust no strange tailor, he had sent for his own, who had travelled all the way from Hampshire to see him suitably attired. And the ladies' dressmaker, who had been staying in the house for the week past, was hurrying from room to room, engrossed in seeing that all the dresses the ladies had ordered were as near perfection as was possible – Lady Fitzdowne's tawny taffeta, Lady Bidgood's blue satin, Mistress Felicity's white china silk.

All this haste and hurry was added to the stuffiness of the season. The sun blazed between sudden threats of thunder, the heavy almost purple clouds shutting down on a bursting sunshine that gave assurance to the coming harvest . . . Thus within and without the tide of preparation ran fast and furious, the one like a fine cascade with a tinkling musical sound, the other a great rumbling roaring torrent sweeping the farmworkers to the climax of their year . . .

Now it was afternoon and Ned was handing the flowers and the leafy branches. The lady took them from him and arranged them in the great tall vases that had come, she told Ned, from 'the East' – whatever that might mean. As they moved from one to the other, filling and spreading, plucking and tweaking to make a good shape, there came into the hall Lady Fitzdowne herself. Ned had barely set eyes on her before.

"Why, dear girl," she cried as she approached, her voice rather deep, and coming, Ned thought, from somewhere about the third of her chins, "dear girl, what a task! Surely the servants are capable . . . What ruin to your hands, sweet child. Leave it! Leave it, I beg you! By tomorrow you will not be fit to be seen!"

"No doubt I am able to wash my hands, madam," Miss Felicity answered in a tone Ned had certainly never heard from her before – a sharpish, almost bitter tone. "Anyway, madam, the effect is pleasant – as I trust you may agree?"

"Oh tolerable, tolerable," Lady Fitzdowne boomed out. "But rustic – very rustic. Leaves . . . Branches . . . These are for out of doors. At Ardland Court we would use roses. Or gilly flowers . . . Or the sweet camellia, you know. More fitting, I consider, to a formal occasion."

"To be sure, madam, the camellia would be excellent – save that it blooms in early spring. As to roses – you will see there are some that have bloomed late for us."

"Well, well," said her ladyship, "well, well. You are young and will surely learn." She peered then at Ned. "And who's this boy – this dirty boy indoors? I cannot understand you, my dear miss." Then she smiled slightly and added – "I cannot understand you *now* – but maybe one day I shall."

She moved slowly on her way, carrying her bulk with dignity if not with ease. She swept once round the hall and, guest of Sir Joshua or no, she was as clearly making an inspection as he when he came to the kitchen . . . Then she was gone.

Ned looked at Miss Felicity. Her hands were shaking. She was flushed and angry and looked ready to weep.

"Tell me, Ned," she said in a low voice, "can you saddle a horse?"

Ned stared, not knowing what to answer. From flowers and haughty ladies – to saddles and horses? What could she possibly mean?

"Answer!"

"I never did so yet . . ."

"Then let you learn, Ned Only. Pray let you learn – and fast . . . Now go and get about your work. Mrs Hannah will scold me for keeping you so long."

"SADDLE A HORSE?" said Robert, frowning. "Did she say that?"

"Aye – she did. Sharpish, she said it. What's to make of that?"

Robert did not answer. Ned had sneaked off to let Turnboy out and found Robert ahead of him, hot and exhausted, so he said, after half a day of trying on his new clothes; after the fitting, they had had to be altered. He should have been indoors again by now, for the time was wearing away and there was little left to Winterpicks before the splendours of the evening must begin. The sky was now clear but hazed with the day's heat. When the moon rose it would be the colour of a ripe apricot. When the sun set it would be a dark copper.

Robert lolled in the straw and stared gloomily at his feet.

"She should have asked *me*," he said. "She should have trusted *me* – not a stupid old, silly old donkey."

"Might be she did," Ned cried, suddenly eager. "Trusted you'd teach me – show me how."

"*What*?" he scowled more than ever. "Who're you to think so? You puffed-up turnspit, you! Why should my cousin even look at such as you?"

"She did look."

Robert gave the sort of groan that comes from a man hit in the stomach.

"Get a move on, then," he growled. "Come on, can't you? Time's almost gone. Why didn't she say sooner ... Come quick to Jenny's stall. If any can teach such a numbskull – then I'll teach you. And never say – never, never say I wouldn't do the best by a sworn friend." He gave Ned a quick sideways look. "Aye, that's it, old donkey. I asked if you'd help her – remember? Help them both – if they needed – if they asked ... It might be that the time's come round ..."

THEY WERE STILL in Jenny's stall, Ned was repeating his lesson for the fourth time, wrestling with buckles, pinching at girths – when there came a great summoning from the house. Mrs Betty stood in the yard and beat with a spoon on a tin plate. The sound screamed through the quiet and made Ned shiver. It was the sign that the evening was in sight and let all concerned, however humbly, come fast and be ready to get about his duties.

From the farm there came a stirring that turned to a bustle, as those men and lads who were to have a part in the proceedings left their ordinary tasks and hurried to be counted. With them came various wives and daughters, ready to help in the kitchen while those better accustomed moved to positions about the house. Every incoming woman wore a clean apron and a clean cap; every man had stuffed himself into a livery left over from Sir Joshua's days in London. Some of these were too big and many too small. Daniel was in charge of this business. He had seen them clad to the best standard that could be managed. If shoes were too small – then let 'em pinch. If collars were too tight, strangulation must be endured. He showed no mercy to any of them – not even to Jem the waggoner, who was a vast fellow, nor to Adam Rice, the tallest man about Winterpicks, and thin to match.

"Now all is to stand straight and still as stone statueses," Daniel instructed. "Mr Kite told me this, and he was a gent much in company and knows the fashion. So see none shuffles and plucks at his collar. Or pulls his breeches-band at his waist. Stand steady though your shoes do pinch sorely like hell itself. And do not sneeze. Do not cough or yawn – the master'll come raging after wi' a blunderbuss come he see a yawn – yawning is worst of anything.''

On and on he went, yet he had been no better than a kitchen lad when Stephen ran off and left his job for Daniel to fill; and Daniel had been an apt pupil, it was clear, of Mr Kite . . .

Around and above, the house hummed. Doors opened and closed, voices male and female called for assistance. ''Minette!'' shrieked Lady Bidgood; ''Henry, you devil!'' roared Sir Joshua. While Sir Athelstan and his lady, with more gentility, rang the bells once in every three minutes – or so Lucy said. She and Mary were for ever running up and down stairs, though by this time they were badly needed to set out the food on the long white-clothed tables in the big parlour – the little parlour downstairs was reserved for the ladies to leave their wraps, pinch at their curls and settle their skirts after the drive. And tonight there really was roast peacock, its tail feathers flaunting above the glistening jellied meat; and tonight, too, there was swan. Every dish was ornamented, every glass and every mite of silver sparkled. What magic dwelt in Mrs Betty's tipsy fingers that none had guessed at! What glazing, what sugar spinning, what fine heaps of fruit crystallised and arranged as prettily as if they still grew upon their vines and their bushes; what splendours she had achieved!

Meanwhile in the kitchen and the pantry there were still herbs and nuts and leaves, and flowers of borage and nasturtium to be tossed and dressed for salads. There was bread to slice and bread to toast, and biscuits decorated with cherry and angelica to be set in whorls on silver saucers. There was beef to slice fine, mutton to slice thick – the joints that Ned had turned and turned in the days before – while on a long dish that he had had to wash and burnish there lay a fine fat salmon, coffined in bright jelly, with cucumber slices and almonds in pattern along his silver sides, his poor dead eyes turned upwards, his sad mouth turned down.

What a carting and a carrying of all these dishes there would be when supper was called and the guests flocked from the music and the dancing in the hall, up the wide staircase to the big parlour and the waiting feast. There they would quickly reduce the splendour to crumbs and slivers, and there they would probably drink a great deal more than was good for them. And to illuminate both dancing and feasting, hundreds of candles set ready in sconces and candelabras and chandeliers must be lighted by tall Adam Rice, since his reach was the longest; as the night wore on the candles must be watched, trimmed, snuffed and replaced as needed.

When the torch-bearing was over, Daniel now ordered Ned, he must stay fast with Adam and fetch and carry what was needed to keep the illuminations blazing.

"See you step slow and stay out the way of all," Daniel instructed. He looked Ned up and down. "You're fairly spick and sprug, Ned Only. Remember you're a gentleman's servant and behave like 'un. Mr Kite sees all at Winterpicks fit for naun but farmers' suppers."

"Yes, Dan," Ned promised, nodding furiously and shaking with nerves. "I'll be at it, best I know, Daniel. Aye, surelye."

"Now – do you get out and see Jem's got the torches. Hand 'em out and be ready to light up. Any second now, it'll be time."

And indeed as he spoke to Ned at the foot of the back stairs, the evening began. The dressing was done, the ribbons tied, the wigs adjusted, the hair curled and feet squeezed into heeled shoes. The chosen jewels had been clasped round necks and wrists, rings slid on to fingers – some of them far too fat. Now Sir Joshua and Lady Bidgood, she leaning on his arm, descended the wide stairs to the ante-room before the great hall. Behind them came Master Robert, looking half sullen and half pleased with himself in his suit of turquoise blue. Behind him came his cousin Felicity, her white gown cut low on the shoulders and set off by lace that sparkled where tiny gems had been stitched into its folds.

As they took up their places to welcome the guests who must surely, by now, be approaching, they were joined by Sir

Athelstan and Lady Fitzdowne, with their son. Ned had not seen Mr Fitzdowne before, save at a good distance. Now he had a view, sharp though brief, through the carved banisters.

Mr Fitzdowne was of medium height, slender, wearing a suit of rich mulberry and his own dark hair. He looked serious, pale. He greeted his host and hostess as his parents had done. Then, approaching Mistress Felicity, he took her hand and bowed over it. She did not snatch her hand away, but beneath her courtesy was an impression of distaste, of recoil that even Ned could recognise.

"Quick!" hissed Daniel. "The torches! I've better things to do than stay maundering here."

He gave Ned a shove that sent him hurriedly on his way. As he went he heard the musicians striking up in the hall – Mr Ransom, Ned knew, had seen them installed and had stayed for the last hour discussing and choosing the dances they were to play. Though Ned had not had so much as a snatched glance of Mr Ransom all that day, he knew very well that he must be looking as pale as Mr Fitzdowne. Mr Fitzdowne would be pale with anticipation of what the next hours might bring; Mr Ransom pale with despair . . .

Jem had handed out the torches. His own flared up and the flame was then passed from one to the other. The last torch leapt, the men, twelve or more, took up their positions on either side of the avenue. And as Ned scuttled to a chosen place as near as possible to the grand entrance of Winterpicks manor house, the first coach swung in from the road and came rumbling sturdily up the avenue.

8

IT WAS NOT ONLY that Ned had never witnessed such an occasion as the Winterpicks summer ball – he could never have begun to imagine what such an occasion might be like. The only dancing he had ever seen was at the harvest home. He had never even set eyes on ladies and gentlemen in such rich and extravagant attire as those who now swept into the hall to the sound of music very different from the jigs and hornpipes of country dancers.

Sir Joshua had cast his net wide among the country gentry and the response had doubtless flattered him. Though the grandest, as Mr Kite had been quick to inform any prepared to listen, might not be so immensely desirous of meeting Sir Joshua – they would come to meet Sir Athelstan Fitzdowne, whose name appeared on the invitation. It was a name calculated to tempt even a reluctant guest. The Duke himself, Mr Kite had hinted, might be prepared to attend – then later conceded that his Grace, though ready to visit Sir Athelstan at Ardland, might think very little of appearing at an establishment as mean as Winterpicks Manor.

"I have taken note of the whims and manners of the mighty," Mr Kite had announced. "Gentlemen is chancy animals."

In spite of Mr Kite, sixty guests were expected. Of these at least ten would expect over-night accommodation. Now from all corners of the county they were converging on Winterpicks. The first coach was speedily followed by a carriage and pair, followed by a far humbler conveyance, little better than a farm cart. This carried a widow with four daughters and six sons; a family both poor and of an ancient name dwelling in a ramshackle manor built into the walls of their tumbledown castle. After them came two more coaches, full of ladies, their escorting gentlemen riding alongside . . .

Ned held up his torch till his arm ached, snatching quick glimpses of laughing girls, handsome men, haughty dowagers and bewigged knights and squires. He watched grooms leap down to open coach and carriage doors, releasing gentlemen in white stockings and buckled shoes, and ladies scooping up their fine skirts lest they trail along the summer-dusty ground. The moonlight gleamed on satin and lace and ribbon, it sparkled in gems set in dressed curls, round white necks and wrists, on small hands that looked too feeble to care for themselves. There came a modest chattering and laughter, as friends and acquaintances greeted one another before sweeping into the house where their host awaited them . . .

The torches burnt low and spluttered. The empty conveyances were driven round to the stables, where their drivers and attendants would find entertainment with Sir Joshua's coachmen. Mr and Mrs Langridge, who had walked modestly from the parsonage, entered the house and now the door was closing . . .

Jem collected the dead torches and carried them away, walking pigeon-toed in his tight, unfamiliar shoes. Adam Rice, moving more comfortably, caught Ned by the arm.

"Don't you go lope off'n leave me now, Ned Only. There's work for you and me indoors – and well you know it."

"I never was loping off."

"Come within, then – though seeing I'm the highest in height and you'm the least we make a sad pair."

There was a mannerly quiet about that first hour of the ball. The music played gently and the chatter was restrained. Ned, stationed by Adam near the foot of the big stairway and waiting to be made use of, could scarcely believe that so many people would make so little noise. Even Sir Joshua's voice, which did emerge above the others at times, seemed less than half itself, so genteel was the gathering.

Through the wide doorway that led into the hall, Ned watched the shifting pattern of the ball. He saw the dancers moving in delicate figures, sedate and graceful, now in view, now moving away as the figure of the dance dictated. He heard the music and saw some of the older ladies seated together, leaning towards one another and gossiping, and hiding that gossip behind their fans. The pretty girls swept across the floor like swooping birds, and their partners, who seemed to Ned all handsome and healthy and vain, moved in the dance as lightly and gracefully as the girls. Sometimes Ned saw his particular young lady dance by, and she of them all seemed to move stiffly, as if in a dream that binds the limbs and numbs the mind. Her manner frightened him. He thought of Mr Fitzdowne, of Mr Ransom. His imagination suddenly kindled. His heart lurched and thumped. He remembered tales told by Mary to the rest of them, of parted lovers and dreadful fate. In minutes, standing there where he had been put, Ned began to grow up; so much so that he almost understood the anguish of all three . . .

The musicians played high in what older times had called the minstrels' gallery, and up there with them stayed Mr Ransom. Was he to have no dance, Ned wondered? Was he considered unfit, too humble to mingle with these guests? Ned looked about for Robert. Might he be able to go to Mr Ransom and bring him to join the rest?

Now slowly the pace was increasing, the noise beginning to swell. The music was louder and so was the laughter and the talk. Soon it would be supper time and then, whatever ideas Adam might have, Ned would be needed to fetch and carry from the kitchen. And at that very moment Daniel, passing with a tray of glasses and wine, kicked him sharply on the ankle, frowning and muttering.

"Why're you still here, you grummert? Get to the kitchen – you're wanted!"

Ned went at once. The idea of carrying great dishes to the long tables, so splendidly decked, filled him with alarm. It was certain he would drop something. What if he should collide with one of the grandest among them, tilt sauce into some gentleman's shoes, pour syrup down a lady's skirt . . . How terrible a trial had come upon him – and all because his master had not clever, knowing servants enough and so must bring in those whose everyday was concerned with far rougher matters.

Perhaps Mrs Hannah, like Daniel, had learnt from Mr Kite. She had lined up the maids in the passage beyond the kitchen door and now each in turn was being given a dish to carry. The heaviest had already been placed – now came the salads and the side dishes, the various breads to be set among the meats and the fish; also pies and puddings, tarts spiced with cinnamon and ginger, to be arrayed on a second table under the window. Some girls, those who had been brought in for the evening, carried jugs of wine, bowls of punch, with lighter drinks to suit the youngest ladies.

Daniel came fast and busy to inspect.

"Very good," he pronounced, almost in the tones of Mr Kite himself. "Now. Do you all follow me. It's for me to stand at the hall entry and cry out that supper be served." He paused and looked round. "Where's Ned Only?"

"Here, Dan . . . "

"Now, Ned. Show thy spirit. Stand up straight and walk wi' me. And when we're to the parlour door, do you throw it widest open. Then stand back flat agin the wall that all may enter. And you girls, come you've set the dishes and such down in good order, then be ready to hand and serve as is needed and called for. Mrs Hannah know the best to do – so what she say to do, then do."

They nodded and murmured nervously. Mrs Hannah bridled and looked fierce, smoothing down the apron over her dark dress, that had been given her by Mrs Dorothea and had collar and cuffs of white netted lace. It was a little large, even on Mrs Hannah; Minette, with rare friendliness, had offered to alter it to a better fit, but then had been so demanded by Lady Bidgood that the time had passed for the job.

"March off, then!" ordered Daniel.

They stepped out obediently. As they came nearer the hall, so the music swelled out, so lively now that it slid them into a rhythm, almost into a dance. Above the sound of music was the sound of merry company, the strange busy murmur of voices in agreement, of human enjoyment of a pleasant occasion whose liveliness increased with every second.

"A moment, Daniel," Mrs Hannah said, unusually low and urgent. "What of the betrothal? When shall that be called? Shall it be at supper? Or when supper's fully done?"

"I know naun of it," Daniel answered, sharp and irritable.

"Better the earth quake and stop all," Mrs Hannah muttered. "Men are devils that buy and sell their lovely girls."

That was the worst that had so far been spoken of Sir Joshua and his wardenship and Daniel looked round quickly, as if he feared their master might hear and turn the lot of them out of doors . . .

Ned moved carefully a pace behind Daniel, who carried a staff of office. Such unreality had now spread over the whole occasion that Ned walked in a dream. He was two persons in one. He was a solemn page, for whom the gaiety of the gentry was a commonplace, and he was Ned Only, accustomed to the heat and grease of the kitchen, who had lied about Turnboy's death and now kept him in secret defiance, stealing meat for him from the master's own table . . . The confusion of it all made him sweat.

In the entry to the hall Daniel stood erect and cleared his throat.

"Supper – " he began. His voice was pitched high and thin as a bantam's, and he was obliged to stop and clear his throat yet again. He thumped with his staff on the floor. No doubt at the order of Mr Ransom, waiting for the signal, the music dwindled away and ended on a fine long chord. With immense courage, for he was shaking, Daniel then produced his own countryman's firm loud voice and cried out –

"Supper – is – served!"

Then he led off up the stairs and Ned flung open the parlour door and stood back as ordered. On a wave of chatter and laughter the guests paired each with a chosen partner and all proceeded in well-mannered merriment to the feast. There

Mrs Hannah and the girls waited, and there, after a polite pause, the food and the wine began to circulate and tongues were miraculously loosened.

NED COULD NOT have escaped, even if he had wanted to. Daniel, Mrs Hannah, Lucy, Mary, Susan – all called on him. Carry this, hold that, pick up the fallen crumbs, mop up the spilt wine, carry away these dishes, wash them, bring them back . . . There was not a moment's peace, not a second to gape at the ladies and think them beautiful, though none so beautiful as the one he best cared for. Barely time to search out Mr Ransom and frown at his extreme solemnity; but just time to make a point of filling Master Robert's glass uncomfortably full and look boldly into his reddening face, then turn aside to hide a grin. Though he was tired, though his feet ached in shoes that had not been his till tonight, Ned wished the evening might never end. The increasing noise, the now less orderly laughter, even the heat from the candles whose flames leaned a little in the night air breathing, and no more than breathing, beyond the open windows, bred in him a kind of wildness. Anything might happen – and it might happen to him – to Ned Only, the thin boy, the despised pauper.

Adam grabbed at Ned's arm, as he hurried once more on a kitchen errand.

''Fetch candles! Quick about it! There's some guttering like marsh fires – and some's burnt clean out and the socket empty! Get on quick and stop doddling – they'll soon not see their faces for the gloom!''

Ned dashed off and dragged back a great basket of candles, only to be hissed at by a frantic Mrs Hannah.

''Draw more ale! And there's a hogshead o' claret must needs be broached. Can you do that, Ned, and no help? Otherly, shout for Jem.''

He could do anything. Mrs Hannah's feverish manner added to his excitement, his certainty of his own strength. As he strode off to the cellar he knew himself to be as strong and as clever as ten grown men, though they might be gentlemen.

He was no more frightened of any one person there that night than he was of Turnboy . . .

He drew more ale and carried it to the parlour door – Lucy and Susan took it from him. Now he was back in the cellar and letting the wine into jugs; now he was carrying the jugs, two at a time, to the feasting. He had been away less than half an hour, but in that time the noisy merriment had increased to a tumult. These gentlemen and their ladies were behaving more and more as their own ploughmen and carters might behave at some country festival; the ladies were as gigglesome, the gentlemen as flushed, and even the older ladies seemed to have forgotten their better manners. Among them moved Sir Joshua, from one to another tottered Lady Bidgood – while Sir Athelstan and his lady, on seats a little raised above the rest, looked on with fair geniality, accepting if not enjoying the conversation of those brought to them.

But where Mistress Felicity sat there was a little clearing of the crowd. Mr Fitzdowne stood behind her chair, stooping now and again to speak quietly in her ear. She was unsmiling and he looked anxious. Those around them seemed to be watching, waiting; occasionally one would whisper to a neighbour; there were smiles, nods.

"Take the wine round," Mrs Hannah ordered Ned. "Aye, you must, will you, nil you, for the rest of us is too busy. We've to clear the left food away. Else the sight's so slummocky the master'll come roaring. Take the wine, Ned! Take it!"

"Nay – I dursen't! I'll spill 'un!" Faced with such a task, Ned's vanity was shaken.

"Do's you're bid! Get on, I say! Get on wi' you!"

Every other gentleman seemed to be holding an empty glass, and of the ladies the elder sort gladly accepted what was offered. Dazed now, Ned worked his way among them with trembling care; where was that comfortable certainty that he cared not a jot for any of them? One jug was quickly emptied, and then the second. He might very well have to run again to the cellar.

He was approaching Mistress Felicity. She sat with her head bent, looking at her hands. Mr Fitzdowne was still beside her and on a small table at his elbow his glass stood half empty. As Ned came near, Mr Fitzdowne picked up the glass, tossed off what remained and held it to be filled.

Now Ned was standing in front of the lady. Now he was lifting the jug towards the glass . . . She looked up – and seeing Ned her face was suddenly lit by wildness and excitement . . .

What happened next was not easily explained. She moved sharply in her chair. As she did so, Mr Fitzdowne's glass, already near to brimming, was knocked from his hands and all its contents gushed out over her white gown.

Immediate cries of horror rang out. She sprang up and the wine ran down her skirt from waist to hem.

"Stupid boy!" cried Mr Fitzdowne. "Oh my dear madam – your lovely gown!"

Word of the calamity was round the room in seconds. Almost before she moved, kerchiefs and napkins were offered in gabbling sympathy and outrage. Mr Fitzdowne went on his knees in an attempt to mop up the wine – then moved back in confusion, as if guilty of some shocking familiarity.

She was still looking at Ned. She seemed almost to be passing him some message and he strove hard to understand, pretty well deaf to the angry cries directed at him from all sides.

Then she gathered up her ruined skirts in one hand and with the other grabbed Ned by the wrist. She seemed to hurl herself through the crowding gaping guests – so furiously that they fell back and let her go.

It was then that Sir Joshua, occupied in a far part of the room, seemed to realise at last that something was wrong. He hurried forward, so that she and Ned came face to face with him.

"My dearest child – !"

She stood an instant, still gripping Ned's wrist.

"Leave me," she said, not loudly but with such bitter intent that his jaw dropped. Then she recovered a little. "I shall change. Pray send me Lucy. Let the dancing begin again – at once, at once! Step aside, sir, if you please. I must rid myself of this – this disaster.''

''That boy,'' he spluttered, ''that abominable boy . . . Was it his doing?''

''Let me by, and the boy, too,'' she cried. ''Come, Ned. I have business with you.''

With that she dragged him past Sir Joshua and out through the ante room towards the stairway . . .

''Is he following, Ned?'' she muttered.

He glanced back. ''Nay, lady. Gone.''

''Go to the stable. I shall look for you there. Ah! Listen! The music . . . Go quickly, Ned. There is no time . . .''

She released him and fled upstairs and he stood trying to recover his wits and understand what it was she had told him to do.

Lucy ran from the parlour. ''Where is she?''

''Up the stairs . . .''

''I'd not be you, Ned Only,'' cried Lucy as she ran off.

He turned and went away quickly, as he had been ordered.

IF ONLY Mr Ransom were there – he would know what was best. If only Robert would come to reassure, to say, ''You're doing the right thing, old donkey.'' And what was he doing, alone there in the stable where she had sent him, with the stalled horses fidgeting, saddles hanging each on its peg, bridles and bits ranged on the walls of the harness room just beyond Jenny's stall . . . What was it Robert had asked of him, that day they rode to see the ocean lying at the foot of the downs? Promise to help them, he had said. That had meant she and Mr Ransom running away together to escape her guardian's greedy plans . . . But now Mr Ransom was not in the place Robert had chosen for him. That meant – did it? – that she would go alone? In those tales Ned had heard the girls telling in the kitchen, of fleeing lovers and terrible pursuit, there were always two of them; and in the end, after wild disasters love was sure to be triumphant. Maybe this was not always so in truth? The bleak black side of such events, that the storytellers chose to forget, was all too obvious to Ned Only, standing there in the dark stable and remembering the manners of Sir Joshua Bidgood of Winterpicks.

These thoughts roused him. He would not fail her, whatever was asked of him. He began busying himself with the difficulties of saddling, choosing Mr Ransom's horse, Jewel, as the best tempered, struggling with the heavy side saddle the lady would need, longing for a few more inches to make the job easier.

The night seemed to be wearing right away. Now the buckles were dealt with, the girths ready for adjustment. Outside and in, the light was milky, for the moon had misted over, so that Ned recalled the threat of thunder in the early part of the day, in the morning, in another life, when he and Robert had run together to the spring. From the house the music sounded unduly loud in the stillness. If the summer were not so far gone, Ned thought, nightingales would have answered the music. As it was, a burst of loud laughter from the coach-house roused a reply from owls and nightjars.

Loneliness and fear swept into Ned's heart. She was not coming after all. She had been prevented, dragged back to Mr Fitzdowne. Nothing would remain for Ned but certain punishment – though he knew positively the fault had not been his. He knew positively that she must have knocked the glass, spilling the wine deliberately, seized by some sudden mad plan of escape.

He stared from the stable door. The yard was empty. No single soul stirred for all were within doors, the guests at the dancing, the servants now busy in the kitchen, the visiting coachmen and grooms occupied with their own entertainment. It was well beyond midnight, but they would dance, so Daniel had assured the rest, and quoting Mr Kite, "till the sun chased off the drunken moon."

Behind Ned, in the old stable adjoining, the straw rustled and Turnboy began to fidget, snuffling under the door, whining and scratching. Ned dared not open the door for fear he might rush in, excited and barking. Any minute, despair and disappointment would break from Ned in bitter tears. He knew it because already his eyes were hot, his throat swollen . . .

Then everything was changed. A far door at the side of the house opened. A shaft of light sliced across the shadow of the wall and two figures slipped out into the yard; the door closed, the light was gone. Time rewound itself for Ned. He knew he had not, after all, waited very long. She could hardly have been swifter. It was his own anxiety that had made him capable of saddling up in a time so short that Robert would admire him for it; if he could only know.

He blinked away the misery that had threatened, and when his sight cleared he saw her running towards him, her long dark cloak flowing over a plain dress. Lucy, also cloaked, panted after her.

"Have you managed, Ned? Is the horse ready?"

"I saddled Jewel, lady."

"Jewel? Mr Ransom's horse?" She laughed. It was an unexpectedly merry sound. "The instant I am gone – run and tell him. Tell him he must fetch what belongs to him. I shall be with my aunt. Her house stands three doors from the parish church – halfway down the hill. He will know where I mean. Waste no time, Ned. Do you understand?"

"Shall you ride alone?" Ned cried, amazed and alarmed.

"Lucy will come with me. Quick, now – saddle her my cousin's pony."

Lucy began to cry. "I cannot, ma'am! Nay, never ask me! Never ask me!"

"You said you would come. You have made ready – you have my cloak to wear!"

"I dursen't!" Lucy cried, now weeping bitterly. "The master'll catch us like running meece! I'll get turned out o'doors . . ."

"Hurry with Jenny, Ned!" Then she snapped at Lucy, "Be silent, you silly girl – someone will hear." She began to argue, even to threaten. "Hurry!" she cried to Ned. "Hurry!"

The pony was easy to handle. Again Ned was startled by his own unexpected skill, and longed for praise. And she did cry, "Good! Oh good, Ned! Now bring them both out. Quietly . . . Give Lucy a hand."

"Nay!" Lucy cried. "The saddle's naun for a lady – "

"Then ride like a man!" cried Miss Felicity.

But with a last wild burst of sobbing Lucy turned and was gone, running fast across the moonlit yard and back into the house.

"Joss me up, as you say," the lady ordered Ned, her teeth clenched. "No time to waste. Will she betray us, do you think?" Then she bent from the saddle and spoke softly. "I'll never forget you, Ned. Go to Mr Ransom. Quickly. Farewell, my dear lad."

She was away, riding on the turf that muffled the hoofbeats, and Ned stood staring after her. In the confusion of Lucy's departure he had forgotten Jenny. The slackly held bridle was whipped from his hand as she flung her head in excitement and went cantering off after Jewel.

Ned dared not shout after her. He ran a few yards in a helpless fashion, then knew he was beaten. Both horses had already vanished. All Ned could think of was to take Turnboy and run fast away from Winterpicks before his part in the affair could be discovered.

Then he remembered Mr Ransom.

The thought of returning to the house filled Ned with terror. He would risk not only being seized by the vengeful Sir Joshua, whose temper must by now be long past bursting point, but the safety of the lady herself. By now they must be tired of waiting for her to reappear in a different gown. And now there was Lucy, if she chose, to tell what had happened. As Ned forced himself from the shelter of the stable he was shaking with fear. When a figure loomed up beside him he almost screamed.

"Hold your noise!" Robert said urgently. "Where is she? What has happened? Her door is locked. No one answers. Knocking and calling – but no reply. Where is she, Ned?"

"She's gone."

"Gone – has she? Where? How, Ned?"

"I'm to tell Mr Ransom . . ."

"Set about it, then – don't stay skulking here. You saddled one of the horses – ?"

"She rid off. Jewel – it were Jewel. One there's worse – for Jenny went and bolted after."

Robert seemed to understand, then, what Ned must be feeling, how terrifying the house would seem to him, crammed with enemies.

"Wait, Ned. Stay here. Jenny's bolted off before this. She'll wander back when she pleases. You stay here and I'll go for Mr Ransom." He paused just long enough to grab Ned's arm. "Trust me, friend."

9

MR RANSOM appeared calm, strong; urgent yet unhurried. He seemed built to handle a crisis. He was also even paler than he had appeared earlier in the evening. In the ill-lit stable, at least, he looked quite white, with a glitter in his eye almost of elation.

"It is not far to her aunt's house . . . Did she choose Jewel for herself, Ned, or did you kindly offer her the mare?"

"Sir, she would've chosen'un – "

"Only you chose first. Well, I think we could probably call you a horse thief – so I'll be another. I'll take Sir Joshua's Strider – and you and I shall keep one another company on the gallows."

Ned could not feel that he had positively stolen Jewel, and wondered at Mr Ransom's being able to have his joke at such a troubled time as this.

"Strider has a vile temper, sir," Robert reminded him.

"I am able to match him. Come – give me a hand." He paused. "What's that noise?"

"Turnboy, master. I dursen't let him loose for fear he bark."

"He'll bark a good deal more if you leave him to guess for ever what's going on. Let him out, Ned – he knows enough to keep clear of hooves."

Ned did as he was told, certain by now that anything Mr Ransom told him to do must be right. And Turnboy proved this by dancing about them in silent excitement, letting out no more sound that squeaks of delight that any mouse could have bettered.

Mr Ransom was into the saddle and gathering himself to be

off. Robert's hand was on the bridle and he gazed up at his tutor in despair.

"We'll never meet again."

"What?" Mr Ransom frowned down at Robert. "Why not?"

"You'll be far away – and I'm left behind here."

"Why, where do you think I should go? I am going to fetch your cousin home. What else should I do?"

"Ride fast and far with her!" Robert cried. "Never think to bring her home! My father will kill her!"

"You must trust me," Mr Ransom said, just as Robert had said to Ned, and had not lied. "You must believe that I know best what to do. For all our sakes – she must come safely home."

"He'll kill her," Robert said again, but weakly, almost wailing it, knowing he was beaten.

"No, no," Mr Ransom said, trying to rally poor Robert's spirits by making him laugh, "I daresay he'll be content just with Ned here."

"So is Mr Fitzdowne to have her after all?"

"Robert, you must let me go. We are wasting precious time. Be sure that Mr Fitzdowne is a better gentleman than you care to think. She knows that. She has forced his hand. He will not want her now."

"Sir! Sir . . . !"

"I cannot waste another second. Stand away!"

"Mr Fitzdowne is not the only suitor in all the world!" Robert cried in misery.

"No!" said Mr Ransom. "He is not! Now – *stand away*!"

He clattered out of the stable and instantly, it seemed to the two boys, was far away.

They stood side by side, stock-still, stunned and quite unable to think what they must do next. Strider's hooves on the turf could still be heard and the sound sharpened for a beat of two as the rider shifted to harder ground. He would have skirted the parkland and come to the last stretch of the avenue, avoiding the lodge and the parsonage and taking the cut through behind the church. After that, all was silent . . .

Save that from the house music could still be heard. It was faster and freer now, as perhaps might be expected when midnight was past but the dancers still keen. Or perhaps the musicians were instructed to play on and thus distract the guests from other matters. For where was Sir Joshua now? Had Lucy been seized and questioned and broken down? If so – why had nothing further happened?

With the music and the owls, the misted moon that was still high and would give light till dawn, the night held all the feverish enchantment of summer's ending – save that it could not be enjoyed.

"Best go indoors," Robert muttered.

Ned's voice trembled as he replied, "I'm sore frit."

"Wait here, then, I'll come back and tell you what's afoot . . ."

But as Robert stepped from the stable, the night seemed to burst apart. The great door of the house was flung open, light poured forth, and with it, as though carried on a tide, men rushed out, talking and shouting, pointing and gesticulating, drowning the sound of music at last and destroying utterly the final shred of magic that had bound all together. Along with the guests were many of the servants, and they had snatched up fresh torches and held them aloft; as though to light the scene would be to sight the quarry. It was impossible to hear what was being shouted, but it was not even necessary; the scene needed no words.

"Lucy told . . ." Ned muttered.

Now they were shifting into some sort of order before the house, the shouting died a little – as if the general had marched up and taken charge. And sure enough, the general ahead of his troops was Sir Joshua, as indeed he was bound to be. Striding forward, half the size, or so it seemed, of any man there, he yet contrived to command them all – though at this stage of the festivities many of his troops were more than merely unsteady and at least a couple had already fallen flat. Sir Joshua might as well have been carrying his sword aloft and shouting "Charge!" In fact he had snatched up his ebony stick and that was raised high as he shouted his orders.

The words came clear enough.

"The stables! To the stables! The boy! Find me that boy!"

And as he veered towards the yard, so his men staggered after him, and the whole phalanx came streaming and shouting towards the stable block.

"Hide!" Robert cried. "Get into the barn!"

Ned went at once and Turnboy went with him.

The barn was big and there was not much in it at this season. The hay was stacked beyond the far high doors and the straw that would be brought indoors was not yet harvested. It seemed a barren hiding place and Ned went at once and tugged the door open enough for him to slide through and maybe dodge out of sight beyond the haystack.

Soon he heard the clamour of the chase close at hand. He hesitated, uncertain which way to go. From here there was the clear sound of Sir Joshua stamping through the stables, crying out in fury as he saw the empty stalls, bellowing yet again,

"Find the boy! Ned! Ned Only! Show your wretched face!"

Now it seemed that those who followed him had become a pack of hounds and hunters. Someone let out a mock baying, another tootled like a hunting horn. They streamed from the stable and swayed across in the direction of the barn.

Robert came into the barn fast. He carried a torch and looked as wild as any of them.

"Go, Ned – go! Go on! Take Turnboy and run! Get out behind the barn and run – run! They're drunk and mad – they'll tear you to pieces like a fox!"

He believed it, and Ned, in his terror, increased by Robert's, believed it, too.

"You – ?" he managed.

"Run!"

Ned ran. He had no need to call Turnboy, who ran fast at his heels. He dodged round the hayrick and then was very quickly on the rising ground that took him to the wood. By the time he reached that much shelter he was panting and stumbling with the speed he had put into his escape. The shouting and the yelling continued, still a great clamour but somehow changed in tone – changed more than a little distance seemed to merit.

Ned paused and looked back. An amazing thing had happened. The hayrick was blazing. As he gazed, flames leapt in the barn thatch.

The new and nearer disaster had claimed the hunt. A few sparks flying and other thatches, of barns, stables, cottages, might catch and burn to destruction. From where he stood, high enough for all to have shrunk to midgets, Ned saw the scene change from one of wild threats and drunken vengeance to a fury of alarm. He thought of the splendid suits of the guests and almost shouted with mad laughter.

Then he remembered the torch flaming in Robert's hand and knew what had happened. Surely there could be no braver, more loyal and true friend in all the world? For a second the thought of leaving such a friend behind was more than Ned could bear. He almost turned and ran back, to take whatever punishment Sir Joshua might find fit for the scapegoat. Then he knew that it was not for such an end that Robert had flung his torch and set a great piece of Winterpicks alight.

Once more Ned turned on his heel. With the dog following him eagerly he went fast away, uncertain of his direction, uncertain of everything except the loss of all he had ever known.

ONCE OVER the brow of the hill, Ned had what was left of the night to himself. The rising ground cut off the noise from the manor. The sky had cleared and the moon was slipping to the horizon. There was the first hint of morning, a quick false dawn, just lifting the eastern skyline. The mist seemed to have dropped from the sky to lie upon the fields in long, just shifting veils. The time was probably somewhere after two o'clock. Ned stood and looked warily over the lonely world, knew he would never return to Winterpicks and had no notion where to go – except away. He thought of those other fugitives – his own father and mother, Stephen and Peg. He had no idea where his parents could have gone, but Mr Ransom had sent the other two to his brother who would, he had promised, be sure to help them. Then it must be there that Ned should go.

He tried to think back to that morning when Stephen and Peg had left Winterpicks. Stephen had come to the kitchen and spoken to Daniel, telling him of Mr Ransom's directions. They were to go north-east to the shelter of the forest, and so travel through quiet places until they came into Kent, to the place that was named on the folded letter. Stephen had not spoken the name, nor numbered the miles between here and there. There was one more thing that Ned recalled. Stephen had named an inn on the way, the *Black Ox*, where they would direct him, easing the last few miles. So the place existed and could be found, even though the finding meant a long and lonely journey.

WHEN THE MORNING finally pointed the east and gave Ned his direction, he set off downhill towards the road. It was a narrow way, winding under the downs on the landward side, leading westward to the utterly unknown, and east to the town which was almost as much of a mystery to Ned. Commonsense told him that where there was one road there must be others, joining it, crossing it, and leading away over the unknown countryside. When it was truly light, he would ask at some cottage how he should journey to the forest. He would be hungry by then. For a second he was frightened again, for how would he get food, since he had nothing to offer in return? Well, he would sweep the floor or draw water, or some such task. His courage returned. While he had himself it was folly to say that he had nothing. He decided that this bit of wisdom might have come from Mr Ransom himself, and he felt pleased with his own determination. He had changed from an ignorant kitchen boy into the true friend of the master's son, and now he became his next self – Ned Only, indeed, but more rightly Ned Alone ... Yet not altogether alone, either, since he had Turnboy to keep him company.

"And see you don't never ever run from me," he instructed the dog, "for then what'd I do but lie and die."

Moving down the hill, the view opened for him. Through the half-light he saw the roofs of Winterpicks, with to their south side a fuzz of smoke, though no glow of fire. So they must have prevented the flames from spreading, though they could not have saved the rick and might well not have saved the barn. He wondered what more Robert might have contrived to aid the escape of his friend. Then he stood very still against a nearby tree, for he heard coaches rumbling on hard surface and knew that the guests from not too far were making their various ways home, leaving behind others with remoter houses; and what strange confusions might those be witnessing?

Here on the lower slopes there was a stretch of untidy woodland, birch scrub, and the harsh blackthorn that gave Winterpicks its name. Beyond and behind this dense mass there were clearings around tall mature beech and lesser oak. The night remained among these trees, the darkness quite unexpected. Ned's eyes were by now accustomed to the open, and had no power for a second or two to save him from blundering into the trees and scratching himself on the tangling thorn. He had to force himself on, for the wood seemed strangely evil, but he knew that the road must somewhere skirt the trees. He was probably still on Winterpicks land and he longed to be away from it. Above his head the birds were shifting among the branches, breaking into the morning noises of the changing season, a mistle thrush, a blackbird lazily calling.

"Stay close," Ned ordered Turnboy, feeling his way through the gloom.

They came to the end of the wood and found the day at last truly beginning. The light, stretching out and upward, showed him a field of standing oats.

Then Ned shrank back against the trees. Something moved in the field, a dark mass that he could not in the half light identify. It moved slowly, big, shapeless – some monster out of legend, a dragon at the least; he had heard of such a creature but he did not know what one might look like. The animal moved lazily, he heard the munching of great teeth, the tearing of the oat stalks. . . .

Beside him, Turnboy barked, then dashed forward and stood barking on and on. The monster lifted its head, turned – and Ned gave a great wild hoot of laughter. It burst from him and sounded so loud in the quiet that he clapped his hands over his mouth.

Disturbed but amiable, the monster, stuffed with oats, turned and ambled towards him.

"Stop your row," he said to Turnboy. "It's Jenny!"

HE HAD MADE the most shocking botch of saddling the pony, Ned saw with shame. The saddle was nowhere to be seen, while the bridle, dragging over the pony's head on to the ground, had already netted one hoof within its loop. If she suddenly broke into anything like a decent pace she would almost certainly be thrown to the ground, easily breaking a leg.

"Now, then, Jenny, Jenny girl," wheedled Ned, edging forward. Jenny seemed to smile as she danced away. "Best you stand – best you be still, Jenny!"

The light was increasing rapidly and Ned was appalled to think how near he was still to Winterpicks. Instead of giving him courage, the daylight took it away. The day was going to be hot, oppressive, still with that threat of thunder. As Ned coaxed, shouted, all but sobbed in supplication to the pony, he grew sweaty and miserable. Meanwhile Jenny pranced quite at her ease, lifting her lip at him – now less in what had seemed a smile than in a threatening sneer. The bridle became increasingly entangled. Any moment the worst might happen.

Then what would he be able to do but run back and find Robert, and Robert would have to bring someone like Adam or Daniel with a gun. And there would be no escape, then . . .

Suddenly Turnboy showed his form. He moved in close, snapping at the pony's heels among the trampled oats, shifting her at the same time towards Ned, who at last was able to lunge forward and grab the bridle.

"Oh my dear beauty . . ." Ned muttered – not to the horse, but to the dog.

The instant she felt a hand on the bridle the pony shuddered into stillness and obedience. Gingerly, hanging on with one hand, he contrived to lift her forefoot and pull the rein clear. He would be obliged, he decided, to trust to her safe return home. No other thought entered his head. He knotted the bridle and left it lying across her neck. Then he headed her up the track and gave her a great wallop on the rump that sent her flying off.

"She'll go find 'un now," Ned told Turnboy.

Then he moved on. He reached the road and went on his way as fast as he could in the shadow of the hedgerow. It would be many hours, perhaps days, he knew, before he found himself within the forest and hidden from Sir Joshua. The road was straight for a time, then curled more conveniently, its curves offering some concealment. On this road there were no cottages, no inn. Ned was desperately hungry and so, no doubt, was Turnboy. They must endure the hunger and travel a good deal further before they dared stop and try to wheedle work enough to pay for a bite.

The road remained quiet for some way, then the sound of hooves sent Ned to find cover. He had one foot through a gap in the hedge when the rider behind him came smartly into view. Only there was no rider – just Robert Bidgood's Jenny, trotting in a spirited but easy manner to overtake an old friend.

Ned stood still and waited for her. The pony came close.

"Good old girl," he called her. "Bide still as stone, Jenny, till I get jossed up."

He approached her in a purposeful manner, and she stamped and tossed her head, though without malice. He got hold of the bridle and told himself there was nothing easier in the world than mounting a horse and settling comfortably for the ride. He arranged the bridle in his hand as he believed he had seen Robert arrange it. He twisted his free hand in Jenny's mane and with a mighty heave he got across the pony's back and gripped her with his knees. He should have remembered from last time not to hold her too hard. She went off almost at a jump and he swayed back and forth so dangerously that he all but gave up and slid off.

"Get about her!" he called to Turnboy.

The dog ran obediently at Jenny's heel, then circled her so that she checked. This happened as many as seven or eight times, and still Ned clung on, and still Turnboy circled and re-circled until at last the pony dropped to a walk and the battle, for the present, was won.

Ned sat firm and saw the world from a new viewpoint. Now it would be possible to move fast through the hot steamy day. Now it would also be possible to be overhauled and arrested, and carried off to gaol for horse-stealing. Mr Ransom had made a joke of it, but there was nothing about the prospect that Ned could find to laugh at. He clung on hard, his empty stomach rattling, and went briskly onwards, due east, but seeking a turn that would lead him more towards the north.

WHEN IT CAME, there was a crossroad, but only a two-sided fingerpost; one pointing southward which would be the road to the town; the other, surely, towards London.

Ned pulled in Jenny, who was now behaving very kindly. Turnboy flopped down at the foot of the post and lay panting. He needed water. Perhaps he needed rest – it was not so long since he had nearly died. The weather had been dry too long for there to be any puddles. Even the long-threatened thunder storm would have been welcome.

Ned looked down at Turnboy and knew he must be picked up and carried, but he was afraid to dismount for fear he might not get himself up again. If he was to be a rider, however, he must somehow learn to get off as well as to get on. So talking to Jenny all the time, he let himself down gingerly. With the rein tight in one hand, he scooped up Turnboy and contrived to get one leg halfway over the pony's back. In doing so he pulled down on the bridle and she went round and round in merry circles. Afraid to let go of the dog but almost ready to cry, Ned gritted his teeth and just contrived to struggle back into place. He settled Turnboy like a sack ahead of him and boldly turned Jenny's head northwards. London was very far away. There would be many turnings before such a distant place could be reached. Somewhere on the way would be the road Ned needed, and he was certain he would find it. Half a mile on they came to water running beside the road, a clear and beautiful stream that looked to all three of them far better than the most generous supply of food.

THE ROAD STAYED empty. The sun blazed and the storm clouds lay well back along the horizon. Had there been cottages, women would at this hour be throwing grain to hens, husbands wiping their hands across their mouths after the day's first ale; milking over, dairymaids would have been carrying home full pails. But nothing stirred. The world was one of open sky, trees, birds, meadows. The harvest stood waiting and the harvesters must be gathering energy to bring it home, sharpening scythes, maybe, and mustering the neighbours. There was nowhere to beg food and nothing to do but plod on hopefully. Perhaps at this moment even Winterpicks seemed preferable to the task Ned had set himself. But he had gone too far to turn back. Though Mr Ransom, returning Sir Joshua his valued ward must therefore be in some favour, even he would never be powerful enough to beg pardon for Ned ... These dismal thoughts brought Ned almost to despair, but not only on his own account. Almost worse was Mr Ransom's strange stubbornness, his certainty that it was right for him to find Miss Felicity and take her home.

It was noon when he saw two riders on the road ahead. His spirits rose at once. The heat haze dazzling over the hard trackway made it difficult to see what manner of person he was following – and immediately he thought of footpads, highwaymen, disbanded soldiers. He could not ride fast because of Turnboy, who was following well enough after being able to drink but still must be cared for.

All the same, Ned kicked up Jenny and trotted on, anxious to make up the distance between him and the riders. After a time he found he was overhauling them, for they were not moving, but stood there in the middle of the road and even at a distance Ned heard their angry voices. One would spur forward suddenly, and then he headed off by the second. The one who spurred forward was a woman; the one who prevented her was a man.

Ned's eyes filled with pitiful tears. Ahead of him, Strider and Jewel carried Mr Ransom and Mistress Felicity.

10

"No!" SHE WAS CRYING, loud and defiant. "That I never will! Winterpicks is no longer my home and never shall be again! Never, never, never! Leave me. Go to my uncle, your master."

Mr Ransom flinched at this and turned his head slightly, as if from a blow. Then he must have heard Jenny's trot, for he looked round.

"Ned," he said, as if Ned had just walked into a perfectly ordinary conversation of which his opinion was to be sought, "Ned – pray ask this lady to be silent one moment and attend to what I am trying to tell her."

Ned did not know whether to laugh out loud or do as he was told. His delight at seeing them was ready to burst from him, joyous and untroubled by the practical difficulties of the situation and by the certain knowledge of danger that threatened them all. They could not possibly be glad to see him as he was glad to see them – yet there did seem to appear in Mr Ransom's manner something like relief. As if a third person, even one no better than Ned Only, might somehow ease the situation. And maybe this did bring a little respectability to the outrageous business of an unwed lady and gentleman travelling alone.

Miss Felicity at once cried out, "Ned! Ned! Why are you here? Are you sent to bring me home?" And the thought was so absurd that she burst out laughing, though with little true merriment. "Shall you make me your prisoner?" she cried. "Quick! I must know!"

"Nay, madam," Ned mumbled. "I run off. There was a great searching and Master Robert said to me to go – to go

119

fast. And to stop any should come after, he did chuck his fiery torch to blaze the hayrick. And in the thatch – the barn thatch . . . ''

''Dear God,'' she said, ''is Winterpicks burned down?'' She frowned and gritted her teeth. ''I am glad of it! There is no place, you see, Mr Ransom, no place to return me like some runaway blackamoor.''

For a second Ned hesitated. Then he caught Mr Ransom's eye and saw that the news pleased him, also. As if, having done all he knew to bring about what had seemed the best, he might now accept defeat and go some way of his own . . . So Ned thought best not to explain how little of Winterpicks was likely to have burnt to ashes.

''Well, then,'' Mr Ransom said, ''you will perhaps permit me to escort you to your aunt's house?''

''You know I am going there.''

He said gently. ''You are riding away from it. I have been trying to tell you this. We must turn back. We are headed north and the town is behind us.''

''I no longer trust you, sir. You urged me to return to Winterpicks. Until then – until then I most certainly supposed you were my friend.''

''Come,'' he said, ''we will go to your aunt.''

''No . . .'' She began to cry, but angrily. ''I no longer feel it safe. She is a silly old woman. How can she protect me from Sir Joshua? I could think of no other place . . .'' She wiped her tears with the back of her hand. Her face was dusty from the ride and the tears streaked and smeared it. ''I will go with Ned. He will protect me.''

Ned almost shut his eyes, so greatly did he dread Mr Ransom's scorn, his mockery that must surely burst from him as she spoke so childishly. But Mr Ransom would probably always surprise Ned.

''Where are you bound, boy?'' he asked. ''Will you take the lady with you?'' He waited for Ned's reply. ''Where will you go?'' he asked again.

Then Ned was obliged to confess that he was bound for that

very place where Mr Ransom himself had sent Stephen and Peg – which must therefore be a place where a fugitive might best go.

"I heard it told how Stephen should hide on the way – he should get to the forest and hide."

"I did tell him so, indeed. You learnt a good lesson. Now pray, Ned, ask the lady if she is still willing to ride there with you. We have wasted too much time in wrangling. If she has changed her mind, now she learns that you are bound for my brother's house – that was my own home – then for sure you and I must ride there alone. And ask her, Ned Only, should she choose to go with you, if I may ride behind and see you take the right way and come to no harm. It is a long way and may be hard to find – hard, anyway, for a lady and a young lad who have never ridden it before. Ask her, boy."

"Madam," Ned began, mumbling it.

But cutting him short she gathered up the reins and heeled Jewel. The mare sped forward. Ned glanced at Mr Ransom and saw him nod, so he rode after her. Mr Ransom then moved into the rear, and in a line of three, with Turnboy running alongside, they set off, north and a little east.

WITHOUT MR RANSOM, how would it have been? Ned did not much care to think. Mr Ransom was positive in manner, hopeful in mood and infinitely, though firmly, courteous. What was more, he had money in one pocket and a tinder-box bulging the other. How would they have managed otherwise? Continuing on their road they came soon to a small town on a hill top, with a church, inn, farms and what Mr Ransom called 'good building'. By now he had moved into the lead and his right had not been questioned. He took them past the inn, where they might have found food, but at the farm just beyond, he reined in and sent Ned to buy bread and cheese, and to ask if there were apples yet.

The farmer's wife looked suspiciously at the money held on the palm of Ned's dirty hand.

"Was that honest come by? I'll never take a thief's coin for fear o' damnation."

"My master give it, goody."

"And who's thy master, save the Lord himself?"

Ned had not met talk of this kind before. It made him uneasy. He pointed to where Mr Ransom and Mistress Felicity waited at the farmyard entry. The woman, still gridgen, as Ned would call it, at last handed over a crooked loaf with a burnt side, a good large hunk of cheese, and a handful of apples little bigger than June's windfall. Ned gave her the coin she asked for and hurried away, feeling her following gaze on the back of his neck . . .

"Soon the forest begins," Mr Ransom said. "There we can find water and break our long fast. But we must not dally. There is certain to be a search. Though Winterpicks were all in ashes, still there would be a search."

He addressed himself altogether to Ned, for the lady was withdrawn and silent. What Mr Ransom wished her to hear, he told to Ned.

Once, before Mr Ransom moved up and took the lead, Ned had whispered to him, "Wun't she speak n'more–" And Mr Ransom had replied in a low voice, "She is afraid, poor dear soul. We must be gentle. It is hell for a woman to act so boldly. It sets every envious hand against her."

Ned remembered how, long ago it seemed, she had called her cousin Robert a monster, and Robert's tutor had answered, "He is lonely, madam." His tone now was the same, warm and understanding, yet very faintly amused, as at some folly that could easily be remedied.

At last they were moving under the trees and the shade fell like dew on them. It was not difficult to find water. Springs abounded and it was clear that they were much used, the ground near them trampled and the water, in one place, cunningly carried to a small pool. They sat under the trees and were glad indeed to break their fast. That is, Ned and Turnboy were glad. Mr Ransom ate little, no doubt sparing the bread for later, while the lady managed little more than a few crumbs.

"Is this the forest, master?" Ned asked. The land was so different here he felt lost.

"A part of it. The forest has been the King's but he has given much away. Gentlemen supported him in his exile. Now that he is home and crowned true King over England, he rewards these gentlemen with what they may not need nor want."

Miss Felicity looked across at Mr Ransom when he said this. She seemed about to break her silence.

"As for example, Winterpicks," Mr Ransom went on. "A poor reward for loyal service, one might think."

"The service, Ned," said the lady, stung into speech, "was payment in advance for the reward. So the reward was bought, not won."

It was impossible for Ned to reply to this; he had no idea what she was talking about. He glanced at Mr Ransom and saw his quick smile, as quickly hidden. At a loss, Ned busied himself with Turnboy. He had travelled far and must travel farther. In spite of what had happened to him such a little time ago, he seemed untired. He was a dog made of muscle and willingness and would not be easily destroyed; all the same, he could not go on for ever.

Mr Ransom saw Ned holding and fondling Turnboy, and frowning a little.

"He'll do well in these shady places, Ned. Soon we must ride faster – but I'll carry him on my saddle, if need be."

They moved on again, and again Ned was sent to buy provisions. This time, from the goodwife at an alehouse, he bought eggs, a chunk of ham, and a jug of ale to drink in the saddle. The landlord carried out the ale and poured it and handed it to the riders. This was on a road that skirted the true forest. The landlord looked with curiosity at the riders and asked a sly question or two, staring with interest at the lady. She had pulled her hood over her hair, and now she held the hood against her cheek, as if it were a veil. The landlord openly smirked. No doubt he had seen other ladies in flight.

"Good day to you," said Mr Ransom; and seemed to gather up his two companions and draw them quickly away.

After this, he rode for a mile or two at a good pace, as if to set a distance between them and the alehouse keeper. At one point, recalling his promise, he reined in and told Ned to hand up Turnboy. He paused long enough to take off his own neckcloth and use it as a sling, in which he settled the dog firmly ahead of him. Turnboy was too tired by then to struggle or fuss; he lay limp and quiet and recognising a master. Mr Ransom now seemed very intent and unsmiling, concerned only to make progress. From time to time he glanced back uneasily at Miss Felicity, who must be tiring. They were all three lacking a night's sleep, but Ned had never felt so wide awake. He was filled with an enduring excitement, travelling in company with these two whose lives were in some unspoken way more important to him than his own.

By a broken-down lodge, long deserted, Mr Ransom turned on a sandy track and they shifted more into shade and the close company of trees. Mr Ransom then seemed easier. He kept his hand on Turnboy, and smiled at Ned.

"I came here often as a boy," he said, addressing Ned but speaking also to the lady. "I was lodged for my studies with a schoolmaster in the town a few miles away. His son and I came here poaching; a dangerous pastime. But we were never caught, happily for us, unhappily for our prey!"

"Is there water near? Or do you misremember?"

"I remember very well. No more than half a mile, I'd say. Rough going. Ride with care."

A stream ran along a shady bottom and dropped over the rock into a fair-sized pool. The water was clear and bright, running fast over stones. Here Mr Ransom halted. All this time he had kept Turnboy carefully, and now he handed him to Ned. Then he dismounted and went to Miss Felicity's side and helped her down. She was weary enough to stumble and he caught her arm to steady her.

"We may rest here," he said. "Have courage. I cannot say that we are near the end of our journey – but we are a great deal nearer than we were!"

For the first time since the disagreement on the road, she

gave him a brief smile. Mr Ransom spread his cloak for her, while Ned took all three horses to drink further downstream. When he returned, she was sitting quietly among the bracken near the edge of the pool, that was shaded and sheltered by tall trees. Ned tied up the horses there. Thanks to the nearness of water there would be grass enough on the stream side of the thicket to satisfy the beasts for a while. Ned saw that Mr Ransom was watching him, and knew from his expression that he was being seen as a good traveller, in spite of never having been so far from home.

"You must make us a fire," Mr Ransom told him. "When that is done take Turnboy and see what you can catch us for our supper."

"My catapult's left behind, master. How'll I go hunting?"

Mr Ransom tossed a knife from his own pocket, saying, "Do what you can."

There was plenty of dry wood for the fire and Ned built it carefully and skilfully. Meanwhile Mr Ransom unsaddled the horses and then tethered them in reach of the grass. All was quiet. It was late afternoon. Ned did not know what Mr Ransom intended next but he did not care, either. He was content. Without knowing what it was he felt, he knew the satisfaction of serving where he trusted. He looked over the peaceful, almost pretty scene, then whistled up Turnboy and set out.

Ned was confident that he could find a rabbit easily in this promising surrounding. Turnboy was a good hunter and would make a fine partner. It was the first time they had actually hunted together. There was no sign of any dwelling place and no movement of man or animal. All the same, the forest did not feel empty. It was a place where fugitives went into hiding, and where those who got a living off the ground moved with stealth; their right was small and when they took more they risked punishment. They would have no welcome for poachers like Ned Only. The silence over all this seemed absolute, but there was in fact a humming of life too intimate to be truly heard. Ned knew nothing of the place. He did not know what he might find over the next brow. As he went he had sense enough to note landmarks for his safe return. To be lost in this tangled place could be to die . . .

Ned and Turnboy were away a long time but the forest would yield them no supper. Rabbits sitting at their burrows' head streaked away as soon as seen. There were deer – but none in sight. In any case Ned doubted that, hungry as he was, he would be able to kill even a yearling with only Mr Ransom's knife.

"We'm fully beat," he told Turnboy.

They were obliged to retrace their steps, Turnboy surer of the way than Ned, who panicked more than once as, for all his care, he seemed to lose direction.

Mr Ransom might have been considering whether this could have happened, for when he saw Ned he went at once to meet him.

"You have been a long time. The lady is anxious. What have you brought us?"

"Naun," said Ned, looking at the ground.

"Stay with her, then. I shall try my fortune. Give me the knife."

Ned cried out in alarm, "Nay – stay wi' us! What if danger come? How'll I care for 'un? Or say *you* might meet danger – and not come again . . . Stay, master! Stay!"

Mr Ransom did not argue. He seemed to understand Ned's alarm very well. He only said, "What of our supper?"

"There's bread. There's cheese – and eggs that come from that farmer's wife."

"Very well. But let you make excuse to the lady for a small supper!"

By now, Ned saw, she had revived. Had they spoken together while he was away? She only smiled when he explained as ordered about the supper. There was more than a spark of her true courageous spirit to be seen in that smile. When Mr Ransom said, without actually addressing her, but as had become his habit just tossing out the words to fall on what ears there might be waiting, "We will rest early and move on at dawn," she answered him directly.

"It is dusk already, sir. I never slept on the hard ground before."

"Be sure Ned and I can pull enough bracken to make it softer. Then we shall take turn about as sentinels."

They ate what they had gathered during the day, baking the eggs on hot stones at the fire; later, when the shells were thrown on to the fire, they watched the blue flame that followed and admired it together. When these simple affairs were over, Mr Ransom and Ned made a great mound of bracken, heaping it higher for the head.

"Wrap your cloak well," Mr Ransom told her. "Pull it close and you will sleep till dawn." He smiled. "That," he said, "is my brotherly advice."

She hesitated a second. "Promise – " she began.

"We have no need of promises, madam. Sleep easily. Your *two* brothers will ensure that no harm comes near."

With that he turned away and went to see to the horses. Ned sat by the fire, dizzy with responsibility and sheer love for the two of them. He sneaked a glance back and saw Miss Felicity, wound in her cloak as instructed, kick off her shoes and pull her feet up into cover. He would not sleep a wink, Ned decided. He would watch every minute of the night, even though it was his second without rest. Mr Ransom should sleep, for upon his wit and strength they all depended.

Presently Mr Ransom came and sat with Ned by the fire. It was a simple matter to keep it fed, for there was fallen wood for the taking. The forest night closed on them, offering new sounds; the birds that had made the evening bright were long silent. Owls swooped, deer trod lightly, a fox slunk by. Stranger than fox or deer, a man and a woman passed in silence. They seemed to spare no glance for the bright fire and those who sat by it. Turnboy did not bark, but muttered low in his throat till they were gone.

"Who'd those be?" Ned asked in a whisper. "Will they tell we'm here?"

"I daresay they have as little and as much right to be here as we have, Ned." He was silent for a time, then frowning slightly, he asked, "How was it that you knew where Stephen went? That I had sent him to my brother?"

"Why – I heard 'un tell."

"Who? Who did he tell? He should have kept silent."

"It were only to Daniel, master – Stephen come to the kitchen to tell Daniel goodbye – and I was on my bed and heard the talk."

Mr Ransom was silent for a moment. He seemed disturbed by what Ned had told him. He leant forward to throw sticks on the fire, and in the glow his anxiety was plain to see.

"There will be great pressure on the servants to tell anything they know. To learn that I sent one fugitive to my home must suggest that I would take another there. Sir Joshua knows only that I came to Winterpicks from Kent. Did Stephen tell Daniel the name of the place?"

"Only it were writ down – but Stephen nor Peggy couldn't read. Only, he said, they must ask at the *Black Ox* inn!"

Again Mr Ransom was silent. Then he asked, "What does Robert know of me before I came to be his tutor?"

"There'd be no reckoning of that, master. What he know he'd never tell."

Mr Ransom nodded. He looked at Ned as he might at a pupil who has learnt his lesson well, the better because of its difficulty.

"You are right, Ned. But I am uneasy. Any man travelling is watched by other men, and those who follow may be shown the way. And though I believe all who serve at Winterpicks will before all else preserve their young lady – there is another I am troubled by. Not for his guile, indeed, but for his honesty."

Ned sat very still, intent on Mr Ransom's voice, with its difficult words; intent on his face that told more, in a way more easily understood. It was amazing to Ned that he should be sitting there at all in that strange place, but that he sat with Mr Ransom and listened to his confidences was very hard to believe. Maybe he spoke more to himself than to Ned, clearing his mind by uttering his thoughts aloud – but even this showed a trust which, with every word, added to Ned's confidence in himself.

"I am talking of Mr Langridge, Ned. The parson. It was through him that I came to Winterpicks – the school master I studied with was his older brother. Mr Langridge knows well where my home is. If he is pressed by Sir Joshua – then as a clergyman, as a man of God, he cannot refuse the truth or cover it with falsehood. It is possible the pursuit has already begun." Again he leant forward restlessly and stirred the fire. "Ned, you are an innocent bystander in this business. If it come to the pinch, however, we must all be blamed. Believe me, I would never have persuaded Mistress Felicity to such rashness as she has shown. Rashness? Courage, more like. The world goes hard for poor men, Ned Only; many, like me, the victims of the strange confused laws of inheritance. Suitors of such ladies as Sir Joshua Bidgood's ward need riches ... Penniless I may be, but I am, I believe, a gentleman. I would never harm her or act against her will in any way."

Ned heard himself say, "What shall happen, master?"

"Who knows? Whether it be good or ill it must be a hard course to reach either end." He looked at Ned and half smiled. "If you prefer, return to Winterpicks. Neither the lady nor I would ever blame you."

"Die first," growled Ned; and meant it.

"Well then ..." Mr Ransom sighed deeply and rubbed his hands wearily over his face. "We must be away at dawn. Get some sleep."

WHILE NED pretended sleep, mists rolled over the high ground and dropped in among the trees. Each wood and spinney lost its shape and became formless and dim. The sun slid a finger over the horizon and the mist became transparent and a little pink. The birds woke, the deer slipped away into hiding seeming to carry the mist with them. The horses were saddled, the last crumbs of bread eaten. As Miss Felicity rode by on lively Jewel, who pricked her ears at every first sound and shied at every second, Ned was startled to hear the lady singing under her breath.

Ned grinned and glanced at Mr Ransom, expecting him to grin back. But he was looking at her with such open love that Ned turned his head away, an ashamed intruder. Then he shivered. What if after all they should be parted. . . ?

They saw more than one forester as they proceeded, and sometimes a greeting was called but more often not. Soon, Mr Ransom had said, as they ate the stale bread and drank from the spring, soon they would leave the forest.

"There is a higher road I think best to take. A little longer, but easier. It is a road, they say, that pilgrims used, a hundred and more years ago."

By the time the sun was fully risen and the mist quite dispersed, they were indeed out of the forest and travelling north. Beyond the town, Mr Ransom explained – which was the town where he had stayed to study as a boy – there was a crossing of the ways and there they would turn eastward.

The countryside was open, the harvest here was well begun. The fields were busy with reapers, men with scythes, women with sickles, children playing by the hedgerows till the time came for the hard task of gleaning the cut fields. The road itself was empty, they passed no other riders. Now they were into the town and Ned was sent once more for provisions. Bread and eggs were easily come by, but the best he was offered in the way of meat was an old and stringy-looking duck.

Mr Ransom and Miss Felicity had ridden on slowly, since his purpose now was not to hang about to be observed and easily remembered. Ned on Jenny, with Turnboy following, overtook them very soon. They rode on and came, as promised, to the turning east, the old road that the pilgrims had travelled all those long years ago.

The sun was hot, there was quiet, no singing birds. Only, very far away, behind them, there was some sound, almost a humming. This was broken by distant cries that increased in volume quite quickly once it was heard.

Ned's blood seemed to well in his ears. A chill of expectation chased up his spine and grabbed at the nape of his neck, the roots of his hair, setting his scalp tingling.

He reined in Jenny who, still fresh, fidgeted and danced. But Turnboy was the one who told Ned what already he more than half knew. The dog stood as Ned had seen him once before – head up, nose quivering, one paw raised; and whining as he stood there, whining and whimpering and shivering with excitement.

"Master!" Ned shouted out. "Master! Master!"

Mr Ransom, three or four lengths ahead, checked and turned in surprise at the wild tone, and shouted back,

"What is it? What's amiss?"

"The drovers!" Ned yelled. "It's the drovers, master! The drovers are coming!"

11

THE NOISE increased very rapidly – a great tangling of sounds into one strong thread, strangely magical, like a sorcerer's great spell, worked on and refined and proved over the centuries; the ancient sound of men and beasts and dogs mingling their cries one with the other, till none might be heard separately. A whole column was approaching, carrying with it a vast cloud of dust. Ahead rode one man, and as he came he called in a vigorous and ringing voice, a cry that it was impossible for any not of his calling to understand. Behind him two hundred or more cattle came, lowing as they were driven, their hooves loud on the hard, sun-baked ground, their heads tossing and their eyes wild. At their heels small dogs ran snapping, keeping them moving, driving back any who strayed on to the tempting green of the grass verges, allowing no rest. And no rest, either, to the great flock of geese that accompanied the herd, forever protesting, cackling and hissing as the dogs chivvied them on their way, rounding up stragglers, keeping an astonishing order. And all the time the leader, dark-bearded, sturdy, riding a rough strong pony, kept up his strange cry:

"Haiptrw ho! Haiptrw ho!"

It was at once a rallying cry and a warning. The surrounding countryside had best take heed of the drovers' approach, for straying animals could become caught up in the surge of cattle, and once absorbed might never be found again. Alongside the roadway just here there was a hedged field with in it six or seven bullocks grazing. At the cry they began to tear wildly from side to side of their pasture, kicking up their heels, pawing the ground, lowering their heads as though they would charge clean through the hedgerow to mingle with the herd. Three or four men came tearing across the field, and their angry shouts and the bellowing of their beasts all added to the amazing tumult.

Further down the road, some chickens, pecking outside a poor-looking cottage were fast gathered in by a boy and an old woman, while a couple of goats and some geese were shoved for safety inside the cottage and the door slammed.

Ned had grabbed Turnboy and now held him fast. He was quivering and whining wretchedly, his hard muscles stretched for escape, as if his herding instincts, bred into him through generations, must have their way. And all the time the great noisy column bored its way through the countryside like a great raging beast out of some old legend, ready to devour all that lay in its way.

The road here ran a little downhill and curving, so that from the front of the crowd it was possible to see back to its ending. Besides the leader with his weird cry, besides the men and the boys who walked alongside, and one who walked alone and last of all, there could be seen a small group following on horseback, seemingly detached from the rest, and yet clearly a part of the great gathering. These were the only ones who were let alone by the little busy, snapping dogs, who were never still, but ran up and down and prevented the lines from breaking, skipping away from hooves and horns, dancing and grinning, as it seemed with pleasure in their own skills . . .

Mr Ransom rode along the grassy waste beside the road, beckoning on his companions, then pausing by the cottage where the old woman stood shaking her fists and muttering with rage. He called to her,

"I never heard that the drovers came this way."

"They come twice," she cried, "but never afore last time." Her voice was stronger than her appearance suggested it might be, and the venom that ran in it was frightening. "Curse 'em, I say! An' curse 'em twenty times over! Whyn't they keep their ways and leave folk in peace? There was four fine beeves lost of my son's herd last time they come."

"They'll soon be by now, goody."

"There's neighbours wi' beasts grazing! Where'll they be found ever agin'?"

Mr Ransom urged his lady and Ned to keep close by him, to hold in their horses, and on no account must Ned let Turnboy go.

"He sees his own sort, Ned – who knows, maybe his very kin."

The leader had by now come level with the cottage. The woman stood at her door and spat, while the boy at her side crossed his eyes horribly and stuck out his tongue. The rider on his solid little mount threw back his head and laughed. As if to mock her he let out that great cry again – "Haiptrw ho!" His voice, loud and full, rang its warning more vigorously than ever, and besides the curious words there was an unfamiliar tone in it, a singing tone, that added to the strangeness, seeming somehow to hang about him and his immense following. It stamped them as unfamiliar and foreign, come from some other land. As the leader neared the travellers waiting by the roadside, he pulled off his big drover's hat and bowed in mocking salute as he went by . . .

"Where are they bound?" Miss Felicity asked.

"To the Kent markets, no doubt," Mr Ransom answered. "They come from Wales – these little black cattle are Welsh runts. I have seen them often enough – but never on this road."

"Poor beasts!" she cried. "So thin and starved – and many gone lame."

"They will be grazed and fattened before going to market. It is hard going – hard for all concerned. For the men and dogs, also . . Keep a fast hold on Turnboy still, Ned."

Ned was already holding so fast to Turnboy that he feared he might be strangled. He held him tucked under his arm like a piglet, and except that he did not precisely squeal, his struggling and wriggling was just as difficult to control, and he was almost as hard and as heavy. Meanwhile, as the column went thunderously past, Jewel and Jenny and Strider became increasingly restive and tiring to handle.

"We cannot stay for ever!" Miss Felicity cried. "Will they never be past?"

They moved only at a walking pace, but gradually their leader's call became less clear. But now the geese, necks outstretched and questing, eyes starting and beaks gaping, somehow eluded the dogs and dashed forward, for they had smelt water. Before the cottage a duckpond enticed and invited, and they surged towards it, gobbling with excitement; and although the men shouted, the boys ran with sticks ready to beat the birds back into line, they still escaped and reached the water. They thrust in their bills and then lifted their long necks to let the water down, pecking and hissing wildly at men and boys and dogs . . . And all the time the old woman stood waving her arms and screaming, as duckweed and minnows and frogs due to her own birds were gobbled by the intruders . . .

Then at last the geese were driven back, the last of the cattle streamed away, the leader's voice drifted back exhausted by distance. Then came the several accompanying riders. There were four young lads, not yet into their twenties, shouting and laughing as they rode, calling out to one another in what must be their own Welsh tongue. Then, a little apart, a man of middle-age in a black suit; and his wife, also wearing black, but with a contented, merry face.

Mr Ransom rode forward, calling out to the man.

"Sir! Sir, I pray you! Where are you bound?"

The man and his wife checked their horses.

"Good day to you, sir," he said to Mr Ransom – and he spoke a plain unmelodious English. "We are riding along with the drovers – as those four young men are – for safe conduct. The roads are full of treachery. Company is desirable." He glanced at Mr Ransom's two companions, who had moved up behind him. "And you, sir? And your good lady?"

Mr Ransom's good lady turned red and looked away. By now, even Ned would have admitted, she looked a good deal less of a lady; her skirt white with dust and crumpled by a night's rest on the forest floor, her hair blown and wild.

"We are going into Kent. To my brother's house," Mr Ransom said.

"My wife and I are bound in the same direction. To Ashford, where my father is a minister of the church. As I am. He is sick and I fear I shall not be in time to receive a last blessing. But there will be much business to attend to."

Mr Ransom now rode alongside the travellers, whose name, it seemed, was Grainger, so Ned and the lady moved after. Miss Felicity spoke under her breath to Ned.

"How much longer must we be delayed? How men do rattle on."

Mr Ransom was saying, "I should be grateful if we might ride along with you."

Again, she muttered to Ned, "Surely we must travel faster than cattle and geese can let us?" Impatiently, she shook up Jewel and put some paces between herself and the rest. Ned did not know if he should follow her or wait for Mr Ransom. He waited, but dismounted and set down Turnboy, putting a string round his neck and walking him alongside Jenny. It was an anxious moment; but though the dog did gaze after the drovers, he stayed by Ned. While this was going on, Ned lost the thread of Mr Ransom's conversation with Mr Grainger. Then he heard him saying, "The lady travels under my protection. If she might ride with your wife it would seem very suitable."

Again, Ned lost the next exchange, having released Turnboy and re-mounted. By the time he moved forward, Mr Ransom was at Miss Felicity's side and was speaking to her earnestly.

"Yes, yes, I know," Ned heard him say, "for sure we shall travel slower. But in this company we shall be very conveniently lost. Who will seek us among cattle and geese and uncouth drovers? May we not see it as a blessing that we have made this encounter? And besides, dear madam," he said, smiling at her encouragingly, "you may now have the company of another woman. Can you not find the chance heaven-sent – as I do?"

Ned waited for some burst of anger, but none came. Instead she answered him in a low and very troubled voice.

"I have put us all in danger, I have been a selfish, silly-minded fool – and it is you may suffer for it. My uncle is a hard, strange man. Nothing must stand in his way, and I believe nothing ever has. Therefore – if it seems better that we should turn back – then I am willing to accept the consequences."

Mr Ransom shook his head. "It is too late for that," he said.

MR GRAINGER was a very pleasant-mannered man. He spoke of his wife always in a fond tone; he addressed her as Madam Spouse. This caused Ned great puzzlement.

"I never ever did hear the name," he said to Mr Ransom, as they were riding together but a little ahead of the others.

"It is by no means her baptismal name, Ned – nor anyone's that I ever knew. It means wife or it means husband, and in this case, as you see, it means wife. She had as well call him by it! Mr Spouse, or Parson Spouse, or Spouse Grainger, just as she wished."

"But you'd never call her so, master?"

"Certainly not. She is not my spouse nor I hers."

Ned frowned and looked sideways at Mr Ransom. He saw that he was being teased, but was not very pleased by that, for it seemed a strange time for joking, with the miles ahead, and Sir Joshua no doubt setting out by now to find them.

"What shall happen to us now, sir?" he asked, not merely for a change of subject but from increasing anxiety that Mr Ransom seemed so ready to dawdle.

"We shall ride on with Mr Grainger and his spouse, Ned. We shall rest where the drovers rest. Tonight they reach the inn called the *Black Ox*."

Ned cried out in excitement. "You said to Stephen – ask at the *Black Ox*!"

"I did." He frowned. "So that is another point on our journey that Daniel might speak of."

"Save he never could. Not Daniel!"

"I pray you are right, thin boy."

"Not Dan!" Ned cried again, knowing it was safe to laugh at such an idea.

Mr Ransom smiled at his certainty, his complete trust and nodded his head. Then he spoke very seriously. "We are in some danger, Ned – or I am. Though I have so happily found the young lady a very good dame to watch over her, I am still her abductor, you know. I have carried her off, I mean," he explained.

"But she wunna *stay*!" Ned protested. "She run off first. And she never would hark to turning back."

"Indeed. And she would be the first to say so. But the law remains. And in such a case as this, the law and a rich angry man make very good cause together."

Ned lost the proper sense of this and kept silent. They rode on side by side, the noise of the drovers ever ahead of them, the dust from the hooves of cattle and horses falling white on their clothes. As they went, Mr Ransom talked in a quiet voice, as if needing to put his thoughts into some shape.

"From hereabouts to the *Black Ox* is eight or nine miles. From the *Black Ox* to journey's end is a good fifteen. We may stay with this company to our journey's end, since the droveway passes the gates of Brackenfield. That is the name of my home, Ned. It is the name, also, of my brother." He glanced at Ned. "Do you understand how that is so? No; I see you do not. Well – let it go for the time . . . The drovers, you see, are a people not unknown to me. But their journeying on this road is unexpected. A bad choice, too. It is too hard for the cattle and wears them out."

It was now that Mr Grainger left the two ladies and came to join Mr Ransom.

"What do you know of an inn named the *Black Ox*?" he asked. "The porthmon – which is what they call their leader – told me they will rest there tonight."

"It is a drovers' inn, first and foremost. But good enough to feed and shelter us for a night. The drovers reach it, more usually, by a different track."

"They are riding wide of London. The plague has closed the markets there, as you will know."

"How far do you plan to travel with them, Mr Grainger?"

"Almost to Ashford. My father's parish is within a mile or two of the town. I have promised to accompany two of the young men travellers as far as there, too – one goes to take up an apprenticeship with his uncle in Canterbury; the other, I think, has enough money to see a bit of the world. And you, sir? How far do you go?"

"A little short of your turn south. The droveway passes my brother's gate."

"So we both travel on family business," Mr Grainger remarked, though with a certain modest curiosity in his tone, for Mr Ransom's circumstances must seem to him a little less commonplace than his own. But all Mr Ransom answered was "Yes, indeed," and went on to speak of Mr Grainger's affairs – where he had come from, what size was his parish, how near to it was the nearest town of consequence, and so on. And what family had he? Some fine upright sons, no doubt, and daughters as pretty as their mother . . . Ned hardly knew where to look, as Mr Ransom poured out these flatteries in his well-mannered fashion, that made Mr Grainger smile in a fairly self-satisfied way.

"I have but one son, sir, but five lovely girls. My son is away at his studies. He is at Oxford. He plans to follow me into the church." He smiled. "These are easier days, sir, since the King returned to his own. Far, far easier. You will agree, I think."

"Easier for many, harder for some," Mr Ransom replied. "But it is ever so at times of change – as I think you will agree."

"Man has only God to fear," Mr Grainger said firmly.

Mr Ransom did not answer. He looked briefly at Ned, whose fears had always been a good deal nearer home.

They rode on at the leisurely pace required by the beasts. At noon the drovers halted, leaving the track for open country.

"We shall rest here," Mr Grainger said. "Have you food with you – or will you be pleased to share what Madam Spouse and I are able to offer?"

139

"That would be very welcome," Mr Ransom said.

Farms and meadows had ended some miles back. Here the common began again, but no animals were grazing. The loud approach of the drovers had brought about a quick herding by cowmen and shepherds and the common was empty. The drovers collected the animals into a ring, and the various boys in the crowd were set to keeping the beasts contained. Within the ring was a meagre pond where animals and birds made the best of what they could reach to drink.

A hundred yards or so away, the drovers congregated to eat the supplies they carried with them, and to broach a little brandy barrel that had been carried on the porthmon's saddle. The rest of the travellers stayed somewhat apart – Mr and Mrs Grainger, Miss Felicity and Mr Ransom, with Ned not knowing quite where he belonged. The four young men, who had so far spoken only among themselves, made a third and individual party.

And scattered at random among all these the dogs lay where they had dropped, stretched out in exhaustion, sleeping instantly and deeply.

Turnboy had become accustomed to the noise and movement of his own sort. But he stayed with Ned, almost warily, as if he feared to lose his place among so many like him. So when Mrs Grainger handed Ned bread and a slice of meat, he ate only half and gave the rest to the dog. Within hearing, the ladies and gentlemen conversed quietly. Miss Felicity seemed calm now, and stayed by Mrs Grainger much as Turnboy stayed by Ned. Mrs Grainger smiled and laughed, throwing back her head in a rather foolish, girlish manner that did not suit her years but made her husband smile fondly.

Ned did not listen to what they were saying, for it would probably mean little to him. Though he was now able to follow most that Mr Ransom said to him about ordinary matters, his turn of phrase was far from what Ned had been accustomed to in the Winterpicks kitchen. Mr Grainger and his wife were from a different part of England, and there was a difference in their voices, too, that needed to be learned. What with that and the the drovers' language, Ned was fairly confused. He watched the four young travellers now racing and leaping and wrestling together and no single word of theirs made sense to him. Even Lady Bidgood's maid, Minette, had had an English of her own that could be understood ...

As if they knew he was watching, the four lads stopped their antics and stood staring across at Ned. One of them was rather fat and reminded him of Robert. What sore punishment might he be enduring now? No friend could have been truer – or madder – than Robert Bidgood as he flung his torch among the hay ... Already that seemed a long time ago. It was as though Robert had slipped away behind Ned and he suddenly wondered if they would ever meet again.

One of the lads was now shouting across at Ned, and pointing. He could not make out what was being said and shook his head furiously, so that they turned to one another, laughing uproariously. Between their cries and the quiet conversation of his own people, Ned sat solitary and now uneasy. He pulled Turnboy against his knee and hugged him, but the dog did not respond. He stared at the shouting boys, quivering but making no attempt to spring away. Was it that he understood what Ned could not? Was he truly a dog from Wales, lost and taken in, and now hearing once more sounds and cries that he had not forgotten? The fear that Ned felt now, the sensation of threat, had nothing to do with the dangers already existing – danger from the law, from Sir Joshua. Now it was Turnboy who was threatened, and because of him, Ned, too. With all his heart, hotly and angrily, Ned cursed the moment when they had met the drovers and turned to journey with them.

The midday was past. The thunder that had threatened for days had blown away and the sky was full of bowling clouds that might later pile up and darken and bring rain. The drovers began to stir themselves and prepare for the continuing journey. The *Black Ox* now called them on and the travellers, too, thought with some longing of hot food and a bed to rest in. The cattle were called back to the road, beaten on with whirling staves and loud cries by the walking drovers and their boys. The leader – the porthmon – stood by his mount and oversaw the mustering. Ned, by now on his own feet and gathering up Jenny, seemed suddenly to catch the man's eye. He shouted something, just as the four lads had done, and pointed. Again, this time with immense vigour, Ned shook his head and turned away.

The porthmon sprang easily into the saddle and kicked his pony into reluctant movement. He crossed the grassy space and halted near Ned, looking hard at him, frowning. Then he pointed at Turnboy.

"Mi welais i'r ci 'na o'r blaen!"

Ned scowled. He had no idea what the man had said but he knew it to be dangerous. Again he shook his head. Impatiently, the remark was repeated. Then as if only just realising what was wrong, he spoke again, in English.

"I have seen that dog before," was what he said.

12

THE PORTHMON'S shout had attracted the attention of others. There were eight drovers in all, not counting the boys – who were left now with the cattle, while their elders moved towards the leader in curiosity, the four young travellers with them.

Ned looked quickly over his shoulder. He needed help. Mr Ransom and the rest still sat together in the sunshine, quietly and gravely conversing, as though in all the world there could be no slightest danger to threaten any single one of them. Seeing no hope from there, Ned crouched down beside Turnboy and put his arms round him defiantly.

The porthmon turned to the rest, crying again in his own tongue, "I have seen that dog before!" and at once a great gabbling excitement was loosed over Ned's head. It seemed to him that each one of them wanted only to drag Turnboy from him, as if they could not believe that any such dog existed unless he were their own. And looking round at some of the other dogs, still only just shaking themselves before getting back to work, it was easy to understand the conviction. Worst thing of all, Ned could see no other dog with quite the same bright white flash, almost star-shaped, that Turnboy carried between his ears. It was this, he thought, that they were pointing to.

Then a newcomer, pushing his way to the front, shouted out, "Ci Bryn Hwll ywe!"

It was as if all agreed, for they nodded and exclaimed and crowded round closer than ever.

"They say it is Bryn Hwll's dog," the porthmon told Ned.

"Pero yw ei en e!" one cried; and again the porthmon translated: "He says the dog's name is Pero."

143

"Nay, it never is! He'm Turnboy – Turnboy!" cried Ned, shouting it out in his rage and fear.

"Pero! Pero!" one of the boys called, snapping his fingers. "Pero!" And he whistled sharply.

And whether Ned wanted to know it or not, he felt Turnboy shake and strain to get away, to answer the cry and the whistle.

Then at last Mr Ransom was at his side.

"Master, master!" cried Ned. "They'm set to steal poor Turnboy!"

"How so?" Mr Ransom asked, frowning.

"This is a drover's dog, see," the porthmon said to Mr Ransom. "Bryn Hwll the drover is his master. How he's come here – never mind. I have not said he's stolen. Not yet."

Mr Ransom frowned. Where was this Bryn Hwll, he wanted to know. At home, the porthmon told him, for on a drive a little over a year ago there had been an accident with a coach. Bryn Hwll had been badly injured, had barely been got home alive. His nephew, too, a young boy, had had his leg broken and been left behind with cottagers who promised to care for him.

"How long have you had charge of the dog, Ned?" Mr Ransom asked.

"A full twelvemonth. More, likely. He come into the yard and got took in and were made well." He broke off, hearing how obvious it all appeared.

"I have seen how like he is to your own dogs," Mr Ransom told the porthmon. "But he is not stolen. That is certain."

"Mi allwn ni fynd a'r ci gartre!" the drover's boy cried, very excited.

"What does he say?"

"He says we may take the dog home, back to his master. Ah – Bryn'll be glad to see the old boy! Not lost at all, look you! It is wonderful!"

"But I think," Mr Ransom said, "since his old master no longer follows his calling, that the dog is happy in a new master. Look at him. You see how well he has been cared for?"

The porthmon began to argue, and everyone there had something to say, while Ned kept his hand firmly on Turnboy, and the dog seemed as troubled as anyone, shifting this way and that, pricking his ears, lolling out his tongue in a great grin and panting madly. Ned was sure he saw a gleam in the porthmon's eyes, as they peered out above his beard and below the brim of his wide drover's hat. Did he see the chance of a bargain? But Ned had never in his life possessed so much as a penny piece; there was nothing he owned that he could offer in exchange for his dog.

"Let us rest the matter," Mr Ransom said, in a determined and masterly manner.

"Maybe best, sir. Maybe. And tomorrow, see, we shall come to the cottage where Ion Hwll was left for his leg to mend. He will know for certain. He will tell us."

"No doubt, no doubt, porthmon. But now it is time our journey continued, I think."

For a second the porthmon hesitated. He and Mr Ransom, both smiling, stood as firm as wrestlers in a great grip, only it was a grip of mind not muscle.

"You are right," the Welshman cried at last – and he was up on his pony and wheeling, already letting out that great cry of warning and rally.

"Haiptrw ho!" And again still louder, "Haiptrw ho-o-o!"

Then once again the great column of men and boys, horses and cattle, geese and dogs and following travellers moved away, while the countryside echoed to the porthmon's call.

All the way from Wales, that they had left behind them almost three weeks ago, the drovers had travelled little more than fifteen miles a day, striking along ancient tracks across the wide countryside to the English markets. They took so much beef out of their own country, Mr Grainger remarked, that there was never chop nor chine for Welshman to dine off. Now, just short of journey's end, the talk was of grazing where the beasts might recover themselves before marketing. They must have time to fatten, time enough at least, to give a cover to the bones on which, it appeared now, the hide was loosely draped. Then, too, the shoes worn for the journey must be cast off, that the creatures might tread once more on the hooves given them by nature. This present journey, since they had been forced by circumstance on to harder tracks than usually, the shoes had become worn and dilapidated and painful; several of the runts were badly lame.

All this Mr Grainger enjoyed telling, but Ned felt Mr Ransom's impatience. He must know it all and have more concern for his own complicated affairs. Time had now passed, time in which Sir Joshua would certainly have organised some pursuit. There were great perils to be avoided, great danger ahead. Ned's imagination was not equal to seeing what the worst might be, but he knew it must be severe. He did not doubt Mr Ransom's wisdom in choosing to travel in this company, for he would not in any way doubt Mr Ransom. All the same, he wished with all his heart they might speed up their horses and dash away, the three of them, to the safety of the place Mr Ransom had called Brackenfield. Again he remembered the tales told by Mary in the kitchen, of fleeing lovers defying pursuit and the happiness and mer- riment of the stories' conclusion . . . Mary had never told a tale of a boy and his dog, and how such a thing might end. Ned thought bleakly of Robert; Robert should have had the care of Turnboy and then he would have been safe for ever. Or would there be safety, now, ever again, for anybody, at Winterpicks? Would Sir Joshua, in his fury, turn everyone out of doors, so that all would be scattered and dispersed and never meet together again. . . ?

It was mid-afternoon and very still. Though the drovers called and the beasts clamoured, the windless trees imposed a silence of their own, shadows were made of melancholy and despair. Ned's mind now filled with dreadful images – of Sir Joshua encountered, of Miss Felicity torn from Mr Ransom's arms, and Mr Ransom flung bleeding into some dark gaol from which he would never emerge . . . Dream became waking nightmare, and from one horror to the next was no more than a quarter of a mile. The drovers would take

Turnboy, Ned would be named a thief and he, too, would die miserably . . .

"Look," cried Mr Ransom, once more at his side, "the yew trees ahead. Do you see them? There we must find our lodging for the night. And tomorrow, God willing, the journey shall be ended."

THE YEW TREES, by long custom, marked a haven for drovers and their beasts. They stood between the inn itself and the farm alongside. The farm belonged to the landlord's brother and it was he who offered grazing and water, with clean straw in barns and lofts for the lesser sort of traveller. There Ned and Turnboy would find their shelter, the drovers' boys and the young travellers. The drovers themselves shouldered their way as by right into the inn, shouting greetings that were loudly and cheerfully returned. Not all drovers, perhaps, were easy guests; it was best to keep them sweet-tempered.

Mr Ransom and Mr Grainger also went to the inn, where they were received respectfully enough. As for the ladies, they were offered a good clean room in the farmhouse, the farmer's wife, with bobs and smiles, assuring them of a hot meal and a soft bed. Ned thought that his young lady looked rather frantically after Mr Ransom, and certainly it might be quite trying to be left so long to the company of pretty Mrs Grainger, who had plenty of laughs and smiles to offer, but little sensible talk.

Ned himself was looking rather anxious, for he was hungry and where was he to eat? Then Mr Ransom called him. They went to eat at the ordinary, there being nothing better in the way of a private dining-room which the gentlemen would gladly have engaged. Amid much noise and robust talk, they ate boiled mutton with greasy gravy, bread a week baked, watery cabbage and rank cheese made of goat's milk – and made too long ago.

Mr Grainger and Mr Ransom sat at one end of the long scrubbed table; the porthmon, sitting next, set a respectful distance between himself and the gentlemen, though now and again flicking an inquisitive glance over his turned shoulder. There was nowhere for Ned but the floor, and there he sat with Turnboy, too hungry to care about eating food which Mrs Betty would have flung out of doors. But it was a good spot for any dog, for bones were tossed down and crusts went rolling among the diners' feet, and with what Ned could spare Turnboy did well.

The low-ceilinged room reeked of smoke and burnt fat, and the sweating drovers made it no sweeter. The shouting increased as the ale flowed, there was singing and banging of pint pots on the wooden table. The strange sound of Welsh spoken rapidly and long, the contrasting English voices, robuster but nowhere near as musical, blended into a sound that was in its way as mysterious as the loud noise of the drive itself, when it flowed through the countryside . . .

The porthmon, now primed with food and drink, leant a little along the table so that he might address Mr Ransom.

"In the matter of Bryn Hwll's dog, sir," he began – sounding respectful but stubborn with it.

Mr Ransom turned to him, his manner the least shade haughty.

"What's that? Ah, yes – the dog. What, in the matter of the dog?"

"Best we take him back with us. He is a good dog and Bryn has no other. And things being bad for him now – well, you will see, sir, how it is."

"We have only your opinion, drover, that this dog is the one that was lost."

"I see him answer to his name – no doubt of it. And then there is the mark, the little mark between his ears. The white mark, almost a star, look you. But there will be a way to make sure. Tomorrow. It will be known tomorrow or next day."

"How shall that be?"

"I have told you of Bryn's nephew, Ion, his sister's son – how his leg was broken and he was left behind . . . And tomorrow we shall go to that cottage, no more than a short five miles from here and take him home with us. Ion will know – and the dog, too."

Ned held Turnboy even tighter, his heart heavy with the threat of loss. He watched the porthmon's face, which showed as many changes as a rainbow's colours. But though there was at times a look of clear cunning, yet there was about him a sturdy conviction and a certainty that was impossible to dislike. He was a man out of his country and therefore on his guard against being cheated.

Mr Ransom changed the subject rather too abruptly, asking where next the drovers would rest, and which markets they had in mind for their animals.

The man frowned and shook his head, saying he feared the markets of Kent and Essex might be overstocked, since those in London had been shut; a good and wise thing in its way, for only a fool would want to trade in the capital till the plague was past.

"And as for grazing – changing our road has changed our chances. Maybe we'll need drive on to the Essex marshes, where is good fattening."

"If you drive so far," Mr Ransom said, "you will kill your poor runts and go home with empty pockets. They are already very sad and lean, I notice."

"If there's land this side the coast, I'd be glad and thankful to know of it, sir."

Now Mr Ransom smiled slightly, saying that he did in fact know a gentleman might be very willing to graze the drovers' beasts for a time. And since they would pass his gate before this time tomorrow, it would be a simple matter to enquire his feelings in the matter.

"There's Christian thinking for you!" the porthmon cried. "When the place is come to – then speak for us."

"Gladly." He did not name Brackenfield, nor the fact that the gentleman in question was his own brother. Instead he looked rather slyly at Ned, sitting there watching and listening with all his eyes and ears. "There are two sides to any bargain, porthmon," he said. "I shall remind you of that."

"You are thinking of the dog? Well, I can only say so far: that if Bryn's nephew, Ion, does not know him on sight, and the dog know him – then the dog is yours."

He had a pot of ale at his elbow and he snatched it up, swilled it round, raised it in salute and tossed back the contents . . .

Mr Grainger said wryly, "You have made a friend, Mr Ransom."

It was at this moment that Ned saw the landlord, tall with immense shoulders, peering about the room. He crossed the floor to them, shoving his way through the crowd.

"Is one of you gentlemen Mr Ransom? Ah, then, sir – was you expecting to be asked for? There's one such asker at the door and trusts to find you. Shall you come to him – or had I best bring him here to you?"

FOR A SECOND Mr Ransom stayed utterly still. As was usual with him, he lost all colour, he looked almost death-like. He needed to take a deep breath before answering.

"I shall come to him, landlord . . . My apologies, Mr Grainger, sir. Ned – come with me. I may need you."

Mr Grainger half rose from the table. "I see you are troubled. Let me accompany you."

"No, no. Ned and I can manage very well."

The landlord stood waiting. Mr Ransom followed him across the floor, Ned close on his heel and Turnboy after him. Ned's heart thumped hard enough to sicken him, he felt stifled.

"Be very watchful, Ned, " Mr Ransom said in a low voice that Ned had to strain to hear. "At the first sign from me, go at once to Mr Grainger and beg him to see Miss Felicity safe to Brackenfield. If it should come to that, I rely on you to go with them."

What did he think might happen? Did he think that Sir Joshua was waiting, that he would have brought some powerful force to support him? Was this the end of the adventure?

The landlord paused at the open door.

"There's your man, sir," he said cheerfully, jerking his head towards a figure standing a few paces away, his back to the inn. "Here!" he shouted through the darkness. "I've brought you the gentleman myself!"

The man swung on his heel.

Before Mr Ransom, before Ned, Turnboy was through the door and leaping at the stranger. Only he was no stranger to Turnboy – or to any of them.

"Dan!" shouted Ned. "Oh – *Daniel!*"

DANIEL stepped forward into the light from the door and Mr Ransom caught him by the arms and all but embraced him.

"How are you come? Are you alone? Why are you here? What brought you to this place of all places?"

"Ned can tell that as well as me, sir. It were Stephen. When Stephen come to say goodbye – barely light and the house still sleeping – he told what you'd done for'm, how he sh'd ask at the *Black Ox* – show the name you'd writ down and ask the way."

"I did say that. Ned has told me part of it. But what of Winterpicks? What of Sir Joshua?"

"Death and destruction, as you might say!" Daniel cried – in the voice he had learnt from Mr Kite. "The young lady gone – you gone – the horses gone . . . Sir Joshua was as near a mad bull as any man ever. An' there was Master Robert, like a fiend out o' hell, kicking the burning straw from one rick to burn another, and setting his torch spinning into the thatch! There was the gentlemen in all their fine clothes fairly begrimed and scorched and ladies falling and fainting . . . None ever saw the like . . ."

"What then?"

"Tumult, like in the Bible. Lucy screaming – for she'd played rat on Miss Felicity and all the rest set about her."

"Mr Langridge, Daniel? What of him at that time?"

"Oh, the poor parson! I hardly dare tell!"

"I must know . . ."

"Why, you see, there was Sir Joshua roaring at'm, a pity Mr

151

Langridge had ever spoke your name, so he said. It was him brought you to Winterpicks, so it was him as had set all to ruin."

"Poor old gentleman. He'd be much disturbed by such talk."

"So he was; sore vlothered. He babbled this and that, for Sir Joshua was on and on. 'Where's he now?' he cried. 'Where'll I go to find the villain?' And Mr Langridge managed that you'd have gone back to your home for sure. 'And where's that?' yelled Sir Joshua. So he said some name, and Kent, he said. Then he took swimey and fell to the ground, so 's his wife ran screaming. But Sir Joshua did n'more than shove him aside wi' his foot and kep' up his stamping and threatening."

"What will he do next, Daniel?"

"First light, he roared, he'd be off to the sheriff and get his warrant and see you arrested and took away and hanged . . . And so for pity's sake," Daniel gabbled, "take the lady and ride fast to that place you sent Stephen. Let you not waste a minute's good time, for he'll be after, hot foot!"

"How long have you been riding? It was bold of you to set out. Thank you, Daniel. And I thank Stephen who told you enough . . . I see you chose Leda. She is a good mover."

"And now I'm a horse thief like you, master, and Ned. So at worst we'll have company for the hanging."

Mr Ransom said, perhaps to himself, "To what straits are we come by impulse. One glass of wine, red on a lady's white dress, and the world's turned upside down . . . Let me think. I have to think carefully, Daniel. No blunders now, or there could indeed be hangings."

Ned shivered. Anxiety and fear possessed him. He thought now miserably, frantically of Mary's tales of fleeing lovers, of the happy endings, knowing for sure that there were other tales, tales that were never told. If she had not fled alone, if she had not forced him to follow her for her safety's sake, then surely things would not now be looking so ugly, so full of fear? He gazed at Mr Ransom, waiting for some swift plan, some word of command, orders to meet this dire necessity; to be away, to reach that place called Brackenfield where there must be safety ... Or might a gentleman be taken even from his own home and flung into prison? Must he even fly across the sea for safety? And would he take her with him? How could it be otherly? So then they would be gone and Ned would never see them again. He almost cried out loud at the thought ...

"What best to do now, master?" Daniel asked, impatient as Ned.

"Wait," Mr Ransom said.

He walked a pace or two into the dark and stood there, both hands at his head as though he would force out wisdom. Behind them the noise from the inn sounded cheerful and easy, no peril there. The cattle sunk down on grateful grass were quiet now and the geese had tucked their heads back. No light showed from the farmhouse lying so quietly away from the inn, as if disowning its robust vulgarity.

Ned looked at Daniel in the light cast from the inn and saw him frowning and uneasy. Then his expression changed and he was alert again and eager, as Mr Ransom turned and came back to them. His step was firm. For good or ill, they knew he had made up his mind.

13

"Now consider this carefully," Mr Ransom said, drawing Daniel to one side, out of the light from the inn. "To obtain a warrant and an officer to execute it, Sir Joshua must go first to the town and seek out the sheriff. From the town he is bound to take a different road from ours, or from yours, Daniel . . . You are positive Mr Langridge spoke some name before he collapsed?"

"Certain."

"But what it was you cannot say?"

"'Twere like *Baron* something – *Baron* and then wood or field or some such."

"Ah – then I believe it to have been Brackenfield."

"Aye, for sure. Brackenfield. And *Kent*. I know that come bursting out."

"Then I think Sir Joshua, the roads running as I know them to, will arrive where we have arrived. The *Black Ox* is a travellers' landmark. The landlord could tell you that few days go by without some enquiry as to direction." At this point he drew Ned closer and the three stood like conspirators, heads together. "Now listen closely – and do not think to doubt or flout me, for there is no way that I can see but this: Daniel, you must ride back the way you came, but turn aside at the next village church and ride for a mile or two a little west. There is the road where the search might be encountered. It must be somehow diverted. It needs to be kept at bay till morning. Do you understand?"

"I understand, master. But how'll it be done?"

"Dan, I cannot tell you. It must depend on so many things. Only do your best. I need an hour or two of tomorrow's daylight and with that I may make us safe. But do not ask me how. Trust me and do what you are able. But if, *after* it is well and truly morning, you come upon Sir Joshua and whoever travels with him – then, Daniel, let them proceed. Nay, direct them here, guide them here. Do it as you will but be sure they arrive. Have I made clear what you must do?"

"Clear enough, master." And mad, he might have added.

"Then get into the inn. Here is a guinea. Buy food and drink. Eat – and then set out. I am sorry you must not sleep, for you have come far. Like the rest of us, I know you must be weary."

Mr Ransom now seemed calm, positive, almost cheerful. His expression was firm, his eyes clear and steady.

"And you. . . ?" Daniel said, frowning.

"I must not leave this place. I must stay here with the lady and not venture forth, however simple that might seem. To encounter Sir Joshua before tomorrow morning could be fatal. I know what I am saying. Obey me!" he cried sharply. "Do as I say and we should all be saved. Get yourself food and then be on your way."

Daniel seemed to hesitate a second longer. Then he went into the inn.

"Now it is your turn, Ned," Mr Ransom said. "There is much for you to do – indeed, the most important of all."

"Tell me, master. I'll do it."

"You must ride to Brackenfield. You must find my good brother and fetch him to me here. Then, even though Sir Joshua come hammering on the door, all shall be set to rights."

THIS WAS the first time Ned had found himself alone on a dark highway at midnight. When he left Winterpicks the first light had been already promised; the next night, the forest night, had been shared. Tonight was deep, the morning far away. The moon, which had so enchanted the summer ball, was now at the same hour near to setting. Clouds that had piled up during the late afternoon had drifted southward and now massed blackly and would hide the stars. No owl called or swished by; no bats darted, filling the silence with cries too thin for man to hear. The only sound was of Jenny's hooves, of his own uneasy breathing.

Mr Ransom had not waited to see Daniel on his way but had swung back at once to the inn, where Mr Grainger stood, rather inquisitively, on the doorstep. Mr Ransom called for writing materials. "Where may I be private, landlord?"

"There's a poorish little chamber above, sir – if you'd be pleased wi' that . . . "

"Come, Mr Grainger," he said then. "I have much to say to you. Your advice, sir. I need your advice – and I hope I may have your assistance . . . Come with us, Ned. I shall give you a letter to my brother."

Between self-importance and sheer fright, Ned had hardly known how to hang on to his wits. He had kept every scrap of his attention on Mr Ransom, had watched him sit down, prepare his quill, set to with ink and paper. The quill had seemed to scratch interminably yet the message was a short one, soon folded and sealed, the candle flaring as the wax was heated. There was a faint hissing as Mr Ransom took his signet ring and spat on it and then clamped it firmly on the hot wax. On the front of the letter he wrote one word. The word must be *Brackenfield*, for then at once the letter was handed to Ned.

"Ride straight without any turn for eight miles or so. At a crossing of five ways you will see a fingerpost. Look at the name it bears and try to be sure it is the name I have written here. It will send you down the second went on your right hand. The second. Any other will lead you astray by many miles. So take good care. Do you understand?"

Ned was fairly sure, but said "Yes" as firmly as if all was utterly clear to him.

"You may well be there before light, unless indeed you miss the way. When you come to the gates, beat on the gate-keeper's door. The lodge will be on your left. Tell him – his name is Cheal – that you must speak with the master. Show him the letter, but keep it fast in your own hand until you are taken to my brother." Again he had said, looking hard into Ned's eyes, "Do you understand?" and again Ned had answered "Yes".

"Now there is one other thing, Ned. If by misfortune my brother is from home, then ask for Mr Marchant. Give him the letter and he will act in my brother's place. He is a good man and will heed what you say." Mr Ransom had paused a second, frowning. "Or lacking Mr Marchant, tell them you must see Mrs Fleet; she is the housekeeper. That is all. I think I have told you all. Waste no time. Be on your way. Leave the dog lest he hinder you. I shall look for you tomorrow morning."

So Ned had taken the letter and hidden it in his shirt, and then Mr Ransom had very solemnly put a hand on his shoulder, saying, "We depend on you. So farewell and God speed."

And as Ned went from the room, hardly seeing where he went, he heard Mr Ransom say to Mr Grainger, "Now, sir, if the lady thinks fit, I must beg help from you . . ."

All these strange matters turned and turned in Ned's mind as he pushed on through the darkness of a night full of puzzles. What was to be asked of Mr Grainger? How if Sir Joshua made his way to the *Black Ox* and set about Mr Ransom before ever Ned arrived back with help? And what help would it be? Should it be all the servants with blunderbusses and staves? Who would be with Sir Joshua? If there should be a battle, what if Mr Ransom suffered harm, if indeed he was killed, as men were who struggled together – what then might become of Miss Felicity?

Then there was the more immediate problem of actually finding his own way to Brackenfield, and of gaining courage enough to batter on the lodge door, convincing the gatekeeper of urgency but holding fast, as Mr Ransom had ordered, to the letter, refusing to part with it to any but the master of the house or to the unknown Mr Marchant or to the housekeeper . . . The difficulties seemed endless. Apart from any other worry, Ned was by this time desperately weary and could easily have slept as he rode. At least a saddle had been found for Jenny, which slightly helped the stiffness and soreness brought about by the long ride straddling her bare back. The pony, too, though she was sure-footed and full of spirit, was suffering in her own way from the hard work of the past days. It was pretty well impossible to rouse her into anything faster than a dogged trot.

The miles, the darkness seemed to stretch for ever. There was no one in all the world save Ned, Ned Only, striving and struggling to cover the distance and bring aid to one he now thought of as his good master . . .

He had been an hour on the road when he heard a sound behind him. Terror seized him, he dared not turn his head. It was only a small sound, but a following one. Too light for man or boy, his reason told him, as he struggled to beat down his fear. It must be some vengeful animal, a wolf, a dragon, a wild boar . . . He urged on Jenny, but it was she who looked back and then stopped so abruptly that Ned almost went over her ears.

It was Turnboy who followed.

The reunion was so joyous it almost brought Ned to tears. This was his dog, his own who would not leave him. They should not be parted, ever. He rode on with twice the energy he had so far contrived to muster. Jenny, too, settled to a better, keener pace, as a pony will who has a dog to run with her . . .

The road suddenly broke into five, as Mr Ransom had promised. At the second turn on the right stood a fingerpost. There was the faintest light by now, or maybe his eyes were accustomed to the dark. Ned paused under the post and peered at the name carved there. He pulled out the letter. He could just see the name on the cover. It did look much like the word on the sign – the shape was surely much the same? With some difficulty, knowing little of such things, he worked out that the word, though appearing once big and once little, looked about the same length.

"This way," he called to Turnboy, sounding positive and cheerful at last.

Then he pulled Jenny round and moved off on to the new road. It was little more than a track, half sand, half grass. It was in fact, he saw, exactly what a droveway might be. He rode on as fast as Jenny would agree to, and now he was full of hope.

As the light increased, Ned saw that he was riding alongside a wall on his right hand. It seemed to stretch for ever and was much like the wall that enclosed some part of Winterpicks park. Beyond the wall, Ned knew, Brackenfield must lie. Soon he would come to the gates and the gatekeeper's lodge and there the next and most important part of his errand would begin.

It was a moment that needed all Ned's courage – all that courage that had gradually been increasing in him over the last days, not yet very strong, easily shattered, but planted and growing. As the lodge stood out dark against the trees behind it, the wall gave way to great gates. Ned kicked up Jenny with a firmness and determination that seemed to destroy for ever the poor trembling kitchen boy, the victim of Sir Joshua Bidgood's senseless bullying, the waif who must die but for charity, however it was clad. Ned Only he must remain – but now he advanced as the trusted servant of a man whose brother, to judge by the size of his estate, must surely be a rich and noble gentleman.

Filled with his new confidence, Ned dismounted as neatly and vigorously as if he had ridden no more than an easy mile or two. He doubled his fist and hammered on the lodge door, shouting out in a voice he did not recognise,

"Open! Open!" He beat again and again shouted. The noise he made astonished him and it astonished Turnboy, who began to bark. "Open! Open!" Ned yelled.

The clamour that he and the dog made between them took effect. A window above the narrow door was flung open.

"Who's there? What's amiss now? What more can happen?"

"Open up – I'm told to ask for the master of the house. A letter. A message for'm. From his brother."

For a second the man at the window seemed stunned.

"Wait!" he shouted at last, hurling the word like a brick from the window so that, almost, Ned ducked. Then there was fumbling at the door and at last it opened. A man in a shirt and no shoes and carrying a lantern, peered through the shadows.

"The master," Ned demanded. "His brother send me – there's a letter for'm."

The man gave a great groan that made Ned step back as if he expected to find a corpse falling against him.

"The master's dead," the man croaked, and put his head in his hands. "God help us, he's dead and gone these ten days and more. Poor soul – poor dear soul – the best in the world – and gone."

Then he seemed to realise who had roused him – a thin boy with a dog at his heels and a dusty, tired-looking pony. A thin boy with his heart now in his boots and despair shamefully threatening tears.

NED FELT SO beaten, after all his confidence, he almost turned away. Just in time he remembered what Mr Ransom had told him. *If the master of the house is from home* . . .

"Mr Marchant," he said. "Where's he?"

"What d'you know o' Mr Marchant? Who're you to come beating on the door and shouting after the poor master, and yelling for Mr Marchant?"

"Did'n I say? A letter from the master's brother – from Mr Ransom, his own brother, to the master! And if no master, then I'm bid to ask for Mr Marchant. And if not Mr Marchant, then Mrs Fleet. So take me – quick! No time to doddle! Take me quick to Mr Marchant!"

Something must have convinced the man – what was he called? Ned could not for a moment remember. Cheal – that was the name. He went back indoors and then quite quickly appeared again, wearing his breeches and shoes.

"If it be some jape," he said, speaking close to Ned's ear, "I'll see your liver's sliced!"

He went off fast up the avenue, that was of lime trees, Ned almost running to keep up with him, Turnboy running to keep up with Ned, and Jenny, hitched to the gates and left behind, calling after them. He might have had the sense to remount her but for the flurry and the man's manner, but for the awful feeling of disaster hanging over all.

The avenue turned as gracefully as a dancer and as they moved into the curve the land on the left opened up, and away through the tall lime trees Ned saw a house of such magnificence that he forgot to look where he was going and all but flattened himself on the ground. The place was twice the size of Winterpicks, which was the biggest dwelling Ned had so far seen. Its ancient walls were as thick as a castle's, and there was a drawbridge which present times allowed to remain permanently and peacefully spanning the wide moat. The place must be all of half a mile from where the gatekeeper strode on and Ned rushed after, and the first shaft of true morning touched it and revealed every instant more of its strong beauty.

Then the avenue skirted a small plain house on their right, hardly more than a cottage.

"Mr Marchant dwells there," the man told Ned. "Which on us best knock 'un up?"

"Better you," Ned answered.

The door stood unlocked and the man went inside. Ned waited on the threshold and heard him call quietly up the stair, "Mr Marchant? Mr Marchant, sir – news . . ."

There was already a servant girl brushing out the parlour. She came to the door at the sound of Cheal's voice, fussed and anxious.

"Leave him rest, do! He's wore out wi' sorrow."

Then she turned to look at Ned.

"Peg!" he cried. "Oh *Peggy!*"

So much had happened that he had all but forgotten her and Stephen. But she had not forgotten. As if he were still a silent, beaten little turnspit instead of a powerful messenger, she held out her arms and caught him into a huge warm and welcoming embrace.

MR MARCHANT was an old man, white-haired, thin but upright. Still wearing his nightcap, he sat and read the letter by candlelight, holding it so close to the flame that Ned feared for his whiskers. Peg had taken Turnboy to the kitchen, Cheal had gone back to his own quarters. The old man and the boy were alone – and what would happen now?

"You have come to a house of mourning," Mr Marchant said, re-folding the letter. "The master of this great place whom I devotedly served, whose father I served before him, is lost to us. He was to ride to his marriage in the country beyond London. He went with a goodly train. They should have skirted London, but no doubt like any other lover he was impatient. They stayed overnight in the city that they might the sooner reach their destination." Mr Marchant paused. His old face crumpled in grief. "Alas, there was no marriage. He took the plague and died before ever reaching to his journey's end. That was ten days past. Only one of his attendants returned to Brackenfield, and that yesterday."

Ned listened in stricken horror. How would it be for Mr Ransom when he heard this dismal news?

"We have been sick with grief, all who are left," the old man told him. "Sick to the heart and might almost have died. I did not know where his brother might be found – he went from home on a strange course and sent no word."

"Peg, sir – and Stephen. Stephen Tuppen. They know him."

"Aye indeed, and I learnt that only last midnight, for I shut myself away in my sorrow and would not open, though they all beat on my door. Stephen is to seek him today – but I fear he may not be there still."

"Nor is he – not there. But I'll take you to 'un and no delay. He's sore pressed, sir."

"Aye – aye, so he tells here. Old fool that I have been . . ."

Mr Marchant looked around him vaguely, as if his poor mind was hardly able to contain all that had happened to the family he had served so long. He sat in a helpless fashion, wasting time, as it could only seem to Ned, letting the day grow so that the candle might as well be snuffed out, hunched and stricken and seeming not to understand even now that there was an urgency in affairs that must be attended to. It seemed enough for him to know that Mr Ransom was alive and well and could be brought home . . . Unless, Ned thought, mad with impatience, unless they came too late.

Then Peggy was at the door, saying "Here's Stephen, sir. They were just riding off. He's here to do all he may," and at once everything changed and quickened. Stephen spoke fast and urgently, planning and deciding, and becoming from one moment to the next the leader they so badly needed.

THEY RODE OUT with a muster of six besides Stephen, Mr Marchant and Ned. Mr Marchant had a brace of pistols on his saddle – though his hands would surely shake too much ever to fire them. Stephen had the blunderbuss that Ned had expected, four others carried cudgels and two relied on their fists. They rode working horses and ponies, for the good horses had gone on the wedding journey and since their masters all but one who brought the dreadful news, had not returned, no more had they. Jenny had been stabled and Ned was mounted on a strange ugly nag that was borrowed from Brackenfield's parson; the creature tested Ned's abilities which, he saw with pride, were increasing by the hour. He wished Robert might see him; already it seemed a lifetime since they had been together. Meanwhile Ned's vanity was held in check by the fear that they had taken too long to get on their way, that their progress was painfully slow because of the old man, that they would reach the inn too late.

"Shalln't us ride on ahead, Stephen?" Ned urged. "Let the old gentleman ride slow wi' one of the men – and us and the rest beat on fast to Mr Ransom?"

There had been little time to explain to Stephen all of Mr

Ransom's business and his present peril. Truly it did seem to Ned now that Mr Ransom's fortunes were about to change; but that might never happen, if Sir Joshua Bidgood reached the *Black Ox* ahead of them.

Now Stephen spoke urgently to Mr Marchant.

"John shall stay wi' you, sir," Ned heard Stephen say. "We'll be but a mile or two ahead. Let you come on more gentle. The boy tells that we should not waste time about the business."

Still Mr Marchant appeared to disagree, though Ned could not hear what he said. Impatient, filled with foreboding, Ned kicked up his ungraceful mount and was away on his own. Stephen might be bound to obey Mr Marchant, but he was not Ned's master.

Given its head, the horse bounded over the ground, the road seemed to come tearing to meet them, to rush away behind with the speed of an arrow. It was as well Peg had Turnboy with her back at Brackenfield, for he could never have kept up and might have killed himself trying. Here came the crossing, and they were over and on to the road that would lead them to the inn. For a second Ned was at a loss. He was leading them. If he shifted too far ahead they might lose sight of him and take the wrong way out of the crossing. If they did that they could be headed for London and not know it for miles.

Ned tried to check his horse, but the creature had other intentions. He fled on wickedly and there was nothing for Ned but to hang on and pray. Then he remembered that Stephen himself had passed along this road already, and he was not a man likely to forget his common sense. Ned settled to the last stretch. Soon he would see the yew trees that stood alongside the inn. Then he would learn the worst – or the best.

A QUARTER OF a mile or so short of the inn, a lane joined the road from the south-west. It was steep and narrow, but it was an obvious short cut and that, no doubt, was why it had come into use. It fell away down a short incline, then curved out of sight. None but a madman would drive it with a coach and four – yet as Ned came near he saw that some such madman was indeed so driving, and with a couple of outriders to add to the inconvenience. The coach swayed and bumped, the horses strained as though they would burst their hearts and lungs. No one but Sir Joshua Bidgood in a mighty hurry could be driving so foolhardily. Ned saw that the coach had only to stick a few seconds longer and he would be past the top of the lane and in the lead. He could reach the inn ahead of the pursuit. He kicked in his heels and the horse leapt forward – then shied violently.

Everything happened at once. The quiet morning exploded into sound. With a furious shout from Sir Joshua, who was now leaning far from the window, and a violent heave from the straining horses, the coach was over the last hummock and into the road, a hundred or so yards ahead of Ned Only. At the very same instant that he knew himself cut off, Ned heard the unmistakable cry of the porthmon. The drovers were about to stream from their resting place and set out on their next stage.

"Haiptrw ho! Haiptrw – haiptrw ho!"

The great shout, warning and magnificent, the cry of a giant who knows himself all powerful, rang out for Ned as never before. It was indeed like a voice from heaven, and it held within it both hope and confusion – for the herd and the herdsmen were set on the same course as the approaching coach and the way was narrow. Within seconds, the cloud of dust raised by the coach would meet the vaster cloud raised by cattle and geese and horses and shouting men.

Ned just managed to hold his now trembling horse. The coach was between him and the inn. There was no space for even one rider to pass.

14

HAVING STREAMED from their grazing place and mustered in confusion in the dusty space before the inn, the cattle were surging forward to the road. The boys were driving the geese from the pond, shouting as they did so. Besides the porthmon's rallying cry, every drover shouted on his own account at the full pitch of his lungs, as if to compete with the cattle's wild lowing, the geese's fury, the frenzied barking of the excited dogs.

Sir Joshua was still leaning from the coach window and he bellowed in his turn. But his words meant nothing, nor his rage, for the porthmon was master and had no love of coaches or their drivers – they had created havoc for him too often in the past. He sat firm on his heavy tough pony and did not check, but came on and on with his animals hustling behind, though the coach was stopped dead in the middle of the track with not an inch for manoeuvring, not a chance of retreat.

"Let me to the inn!" Sir Joshua shouted. "Get off the road, you villain, and take your beasts with you! Who are you to prevent a gentleman getting about his lawful business! Out of my way!"

The porthmon was right up to the coach now, with all the herd pressing behind him, horns tossing, eyes wild and bloodshot, hooves beating on the hard dry road. Then the coach horses began to rear, so that the coachman shouted, too, as the traces threatened to break – while over all the noise and confusion the dust swirled like a fog, out of which the porthmon's mocking face appeared before Sir Joshua.

"I greatly fear you must be damaged, sir," he cried, bowing from the saddle, grinning over his beard. "Your horses and your fine coach, sir! We must ride clean over you, sir. There's no other road, see! Best move yourself, sir, and quick about it, sir, I'd advise."

Ned slid from the saddle and let his horse go, trusting to its own good sense to get out of the way. On foot he could squeeze by the tumult and reach the inn – always supposing the cattle did not knock him down and trample him. Then he saw there was a better way – a break in the hedge that would let him into the field that lay alongside the inn.

He shot forward as fast as he could. By ill-chance the gap in the hedge was precisely alongside the coach door. Sir Joshua hung out of the window, still shouting and protesting, while his coachman, despairing of escape, hit out at the cattle with his great whip, and even took a swipe at the porthmon himself.

"Boy!" roared Sir Joshua.

Ned paused just long enough to grin over his shoulder at his one-time master, and then he was away. He was just aware that Stephen had arrived with Mr Marchant and the rest to add to the confusion. Then he realised, too, that he had shown Sir Joshua a way to the inn, for he had hauled himself from the coach and was racing after with quite astonishing agility.

As Ned reached the inn, still ahead, the landlord and the servants were adding their voices to the rumpus – the landlord attempting by sharp orders to bring some sense to the chaos, the servants more inclined to roar with laughter. Somewhere among all that sea of people, Ned caught sight of Mr Grainger near the inn door, then of his wife, for once not smiling widely but trying to pull him indoors for safety.

Then, on the very threshold, Ned saw Mr Ransom – and the lady.

At the sight of her Ned's heart could have burst with relief. Not only that she was there still safe, whatever trouble might yet be to come, not only that she had somehow smoothed her crumpled, travel-worn clothes and dressed her hair so charmingly that she looked twice as beautiful – but that she was smiling. The extraordinary scene she looked out upon did not disturb her. All strain was gone from her face, from her manner. Happiness seemed to cloud around her as positively as the great cloud of dust that hung over the struggling herd, the frightened horses, the shouting men. She stepped out as lightly and merrily as any other carefree girl. In one hand she carried a posy of wild honeysuckle while her other hand was held by Mr Ransom.

Ned forgot Sir Joshua on his heels. He forgot everything but that she was happy again, that something had happened to banish her fears and touch her with radiance. He ran forward as fast as his weariness would let him, calling as he went –

"Sir! Lady! Master – I'm back!"

Mr Ransom cried out at once and moved towards him.

"Ned! God bless you! Have you brought my brother?"

Before Ned could answer this terrible question, Sir Joshua reached them and hurled himself at Mr Ransom, catching him by his neck-cloth and ready to strangle him if he had had the strength.

"Now see what shall come to you, blackguard!" he cried with such absurd ferocity for his size that Mr Ransom seemed ready to laugh out loud. "The law is with me! The law shall take its course! Be sure your time is running out!" He looked back towards the stranded coach and shouted furiously, "Where are you, you lout? Bring the warrant!"

The coach at this moment overturned, the traces snapped, the horses ran wild among all the rest. The cattle pushed and shoved and even clambered over the obstruction in their frantic need to get away, shattering the windows and catching themselves dangerously on the broken wheels, even becoming entangled in the ruin, their legs through splintered windows and panels decorated with Sir Joshua's coat of arms. And among the terrifying, mangling mass of beasts and men, Ned saw Jem and Adam from Winterpicks, hauling out a portly fellow carrying a paper which he waved as if it were a flag, crying as he did so, in a feeble voice, "In the name of the law ... Arrest ... Arrest that man ..." before collapsing unconscious.

"My brother, Ned?" Mr Ransom said, easily holding off Sir Joshua – trying, indeed, to calm him, as was also his niece, but he was past all reason. At any moment he might surely fall to the ground in an apoplexy.

"Mr Marchant," Ned said. "Mr Marchant is come, sir – wi' Stephen Tuppen . . ."

"Yes, yes – I see him coming!" Mr Ransom cried. And said to his lady, "Look, my dear – this is one of the best old gentlemen I have ever known. He will set all to rights and good sense." He put his hand on Sir Joshua's arm and had it furiously struck away. "Now, Sir Joshua, I beg you . . . Here is my brother's steward. Speak with him, sir. Listen to him . . ."

Sir Joshua only stretched out and grabbed his niece by the wrist, crying in tones of positive anguish.

"Leave this man! He is a criminal and must hang. What have you brought about, foolish girl? You have lost Mr Fitzdowne! You have thrown away your reputation! You will die unwed! You have ruined yourself and all of us – we are all disgraced by your wickedness!"

"Hush," she said. "Oh no, no – it is not as you suppose, sir. You have been a tyrant to me, but I can forgive you."

"*You* forgive?" He groaned so deeply that Ned felt almost sorry for him.

"Why, sir," she said, smiling now, "you tell me I must die unwed – but that is not possible. Pray ask Mr Grainger, there, what he may tell you of that."

Mr Grainger, who had all this time resisted his wife's entreaties to move away from the disgraceful scene, answered instantly.

"The lady speaks truly," he said. "I am a minister of the church, sir. It has been my happiness this day to unite this lady and this gentleman in holy matrimony."

Now at last Sir Joshua was silenced. He stared pitifully from one to the other, then turned away. With no dignity, no shred of pomposity, no meanest echo of his usual self, he tottered a few steps and sank down on the stone mounting-block under the swinging inn sign. At that the first silence fell on them all –

even the herd had somehow extricated itself and begun to shift away. The bride would have moved quickly to comfort her uncle, her own happiness was too great for her to enjoy his wretchedness – but her husband held her back, shaking his head.

Now, as the cattle contrived to move on down the road, many bleeding from broken glass and shattered wood, the dust began to settle a little. Then came the porthmon's cry again, that somehow made nonsense of all the other clamour, so ancient was it, too ancient for any to know when first it had sounded; and too urgent ever to be denied . . .

Mr Ransom was greeting and embracing Mr Marchant, catching his arm and drawing him forward to the others, with Ned following as if by right, the messenger who had brought all together.

Mr Marchant then spoke in a low voice and Ned knew what he must be saying. He looked anxiously at Mr Ransom and saw his expression change to one of shock and distress.

"My brother? My own brother, did you say?"

Mr Marchant then seemed to gather himself. He stood upright and cleared his throat and then his voice came with some power, as if in acknowledgement of a solemn moment.

"You must come home," he said. "Alas, it is true – he is dead and leaves no son to take his place. That place is now yours. Come home at once to Brackenfield, my lord."

TOO SOUNDLY SLEEPING for dreams, Ned woke at last. He stretched in the straw and, without opening his eyes, smiled widely. He thought of the first time he had seen Mr Ransom, when he came to the kitchen and said, "He is very thin." Ned had been thin then in more ways than the fleshly way. His whole life had been thin, his future thin; his thoughts so thin they barely existed. Mr Ransom had set Ned's mind turning as surely as he and the dog had sent the spit wheels spinning . . .

Stephen had settled Ned in the good straw in the loft as early as yesterday's dusk, and he had barely stirred since.

Cockcrow had roused him, but only to sleep again instantly. There was another there, however, to fidget and scratch, to make the bed one way, then unmake it and make it another. Turnboy should have been just as exhausted as Ned was, but he had recovered a great deal sooner, having been fed by Peggy and then given a place to curl up comfortably. Ned could have slept on a proper bed in the cottage where Peg and Stephen lived, but he had preferred what he knew – mostly because it was what Turnboy knew.

So there they were in the stable loft together and what was to come next Ned could only guess at. He thought of those left at Winterpicks, of how Sir Joshua would return there and the old life begin again. But could it ever be the same? Could Sir Joshua himself ever be the same again – for a dream had come true for him, too. "My niece, Lady Brackenfield . . ." He would surely almost swoon with delight when he spoke of her. Stephen had said that guardians of rich young ladies stood to gain greatly when a good marriage was cleverly arranged – such as Sir Joshua had hoped for in the case of Mr Fitzdowne. That could not happen now, for her guardianship was at an end. Mistress Felicity was no longer a rich ward but a rich man's wife – she was 'my niece, the countess', and there was also 'her husband, the earl'. If he had lost he had certainly gained in his own self-importance. Perhaps, therefore, in kindness? Perhaps . . . Mr Grainger had talked long and earnestly with the distressed Sir Joshua before bidding them all farewell and going on his own way with Madam Spouse. Sir Joshua might just remember some of the things that had been said . . .

The rain had poured down in the night, loosed at last upon the waiting countryside. The morning was washed clean, the dust of yesterday's tumult forgotten. It was still early when Ned woke, and he crept from the stable loft with Turnboy and moved cautiously about the strangeness of Brackenfield. The sun was on the house, and the park stretched widely to more distant pastureland. There the home farm would be, Ned thought, and there, too, the drovers rested as promised, their herds on good grass, with barns and outbuildings for their own accommodation.

Ned stood looking across to the fields. There was no sound save of blackbird and robin, pippit and lark, for other birds were past their best voice. Without much wanting to, since he knew that was still a problem to be solved, Ned moved slowly towards the grazing. He stood looking across to the fields and the now quiet cattle, peaceful at last in lush grass, their black hides sharp against the green. Looking back to the farm yard he saw the geese penned alongside a fair pond, and heard their contented conversational gobble. Then further still, he could eye the farm buildings, richly clustered, speaking of prosperity and good labour.

Then, without wanting to, he saw the porthmon, standing by a barn door, watching him.

The porthmon called to someone inside the barn, making a beckoning with his head. A boy came from the barn and joined him. They both stood, staring across at Ned, the porthmon's hand on the boy's shoulder, the boy still and silent beside him. Then the porthmon spoke, leaning down to his companion. The boy shook his head and kicked at the ground. The porthmon straightened himself. Shoving the boy ahead of him, he walked towards Ned as he stood by the field gate.

"A fine day," he said, his voice, with its singing tone, sounding as always the least bit mocking. "Here is Bryn Hwll's nephew, Ion Thomas. He has been a year away from us while his leg was mending. He knows English now." Then he said to the boy, "Well now, Ion, what have you to say?" And smiling at Ned, he said, "He knows how to talk with you. You can be friends . . . Come now, Ion bach – say out what you must."

Ion looked at Ned carefully. He was a sandy boy with pale lashes, and his eyes were very blue. He looked under his sandy brows at Ned and half smiled.

Ned did not smile back for he knew what was coming. He stood stiff and wary, uncertain how he would meet the problem.

When Ion spoke, again prodded by the porthmon, he said first in Welsh, as others has done, pointing at Turnboy,

"Pero yw ei enw e."

Ned did not answer. He shoved Turnboy behind his heel and stared at Ion.

"His name is Pero," Ion said. "He is my Uncle Bryn's dog."

"He's mine," said Ned. He growled it, like a dog himself.

Ion was roused. He snapped his fingers and shouted – "Pero! Pero! Here, boy! Come, Pero!" Then he ran a few yards and called again. "Pero, Pero! Here, Pero!"

Turnboy shot out from behind Ned's heel. He rushed after Ion, barking and bouncing. The boy ran in ever wider circles and the dog ran after, wild with excitement, eyes bright, tail up. Ion ran and ran. He rushed towards the farm yard, then ran fast along the grass towards the house. The faster he went, the closer Turnboy followed . . .

Then suddenly the dog skidded to a halt. He stood for a second, ears pricked, tongue lolling – then he spun about and ran back fast, faster, until he reached Ned at the gate. With a triumphant look at the porthmon, Ned grabbed the dog and swung him up and held him lovingly.

"He's mine," he said.

But he knew, and it was in the porthmon's face, that nothing had been settled. Over the next days, when Ned was being cared for by Peg and Stephen, the problem remained; for the dog ran first to one boy, then to the other; and one night he was not in the stable with Ned but in the barn with Ion. Ned groaned with fear that he must lose him.

Each day at one time or another, the porthmon took trouble to speak with both boys. His manner was easy enough but with a kind of stubborn determination to it. He spoke long about the cattle and the drive over the miles from west to east – of what was seen, who might be met, the pleasure of the open life, free of all but the need to reach the journey's good end. Soon half the drovers would start the homeward trail, while the rest saw these beasts, fattened by then, to market. The drovers' boys would stay with them for they were learning their trade. But Ion would go home with those whose job it was to muster the next herd for driving.

At last the porthmon said to Ion, having been long about relating all this,

"Say what you were going to say, boyo."

"Beth am ddod 'nol gyda ni'?" said Ion, grinning at Ned, teasing him because he could not understand, but frowned and fidgeted in annoyance.

"What does he say?" he demanded, scowling.

Ion spoke for himself. "Why not come back with us? Then the dog shall have both."

Ned stared at him hard and Ion stared back unblinking. Then in his imagination Ned heard the strange calling of the porthmon that ranged echoing over the wide countryside, the extraordinary noise of the following animals, the shouts of the men, the whistling of the boys. He could be one of them. They would travel miles together, moving into distant places, always slow and steady, chucking the miles over their shoulders to await their return, skirting towns, fording rivers . . .

Ned turned and began to walk away, not knowing where he would go or how he might be rid of the idea that the porthmon had dropped so casually into his thoughts. He knew that Turnboy came after him, then paused and looked back to Ion. And then, after perhaps a minute, he found Ion walking beside him and the dog running about them, content and busy.

Ned looked briefly at Ion and very briefly smiled.

MISS FELICITY – her ladyship – cried out in dismay.

"But, Ned, you have been so much with us. Will you leave us now? Do you not remember – you were to work in my garden and care for my flowers – and Turnboy was to have a fine leather collar to make him king of all the dogs?"

"His name is Pero," answered Ned.

"And a good name, too," Mr Ransom – his lordship – said. "*Turnboy* speaks only of unhappy times when he was worked almost to death."

174

"He is Pero. He is Bryn Hwll's dog. Ion must take 'un home."

"You shall have another dog," said her ladyship quickly. "I will give you a fine swift greyhound, if you choose – for I know what I owe, though some might think the debt of no account." She smiled at Ned and seemed to plead. "Stay with us here and you shall always be cared for. My cousin Robert will come to visit and you shall be friends again, as in the old days."

"Let him go, Ned – and take the greyhound!" said his lordship, smiling at his lady who was so sweet and kind.

They stood there side by side in the sunny garden, and Ned did remember how she had promised him he should work in such a place, and how Turnboy should be king of all the dogs. It had seemed such a distant promise and yet now it was as if it had come to fruit too soon. Like Turnboy himself, Ned felt the need to be gone. To come back – yes, to come back, but now to be gone to look upon the curious turning of the world he knew so little.

"I mun go," he said, mumbling it, staring at the ground in case the soft pleading of the lady, the gentleman's generous and friendly smile might weaken what seemed to him a great purpose. Then at last hesitation left him and he looked up steadily. He knew that he had grown to be his own master. "Mun go wi' 'em," he said. "Both us mun go."

FOUR DROVERS, three youngish, one old; Ned and Ion; seven dogs including Pero. It would be a quiet journey compared with the only other Ned had known; but he would know more in the future, he would come this way again, with beasts in company and the dogs running alongside. There might be sheep, pigs – there was no knowing.

The men sang a lot as they went, and Ion joined in easily. In time, Ned would learn how. And he thought of Robert singing as they took their way towards the glittering sea. Robert seemed very far from him now, whatever her ladyship had promised . . . Now they slept under the stars, ate when there was food to be got in whatever fashion. When it rained they got wet, when the sun came out they soon dried. Hour by hour Ion had more to say, telling of the cottage where he had been left to mend his leg, how the cottage woman and her husband had cared for him but given him too little to eat. He said he would soon have Ned speaking Welsh, like any decent fellow. By the evening of the second day neither of them seemed able to stop talking.

That night they were on high ground, like the downs above Winterpicks, which lay somewhere over to the south-west even though Ned was no longer there to know it. The night was fine, but with a wisp of autumn, for they were now into September. They sheltered in a useful quarry. It faced north-eastward, and that way the sky was immensely and mysteriously red.

"House on fire!" cried Ion. He repeated it in Welsh to the old man, who shook his head and answered in the same tongue. "He says that's no mere house, Ned. Maybe all of London's afire!" He pointed in excitement. "The cottage woman's husband told me London lies that way!"

They stared and stared as the great flaring light rose and fell. When morning came the sky was filled with enormous smoke. Could a whole city burn? No one knew.

They were bound to leave that problem unanswered and get on their way. There was far to go. Often they looked back and for many miles the smoke hurled itself across the sky; at dark, though they were far away, the sky still glowed.

Up along the ridge of the downs the world seemed spread ahead and behind in all its huge mystery. This was no dallying life that Ned had chosen and all the time the great views changed, sometimes to roofs and spires, sometimes to broad rivers, even to the sea. They forgot about fires and smoke. The men sang and shouted, their dogs ran at their heels. And Pero ran at the heels first of Ion, then of Ned; first of Ned, then of Ion . . .